"I like listening to you talk. I like how you think, too."

The words were offered slowly, softly. A declaration of admiration. At least.

Or so her heart seemed to think. It flip-flopped, sending a sharp blade of desire down through her most feminine places.

What was she doing?

Ryan leaned forward. Slowly. Deliberating. Coming closer.

Audrey watched, frozen as she waited. There was no thought of action, of should and shouldn'ts, wants or not wants. No thought of any moment that came before, or any that might come after.

His lips covered hers, his hands coming up behind her, pressing her against him, and as she melted into his embrace, she knew that she was going to break her own rules.

Dear Reader,

I have to warn you about Ryan. He's set in his ways. Okay, well, this *is* a warning so I'll just say it–he's rigid. He knows what he knows. He believes what he believes and that's that. He has plans, a respected position as a special crimes detective with the Columbus police force, and a cat. No one tells him what to do. He lives by his instincts, which have saved lives. He works nights by choice so that he can keep his distance from the rest of the living world. His parents all respect him. (He has two sets of them, biological and adoptive.) And worst of all, Ryan is only twenty-two. But if you're anything like me, you're going to forgive him. And love him anyway.

Warning number two. Audrey isn't twenty-two.

Warning number three. This story has some material not intended for young readers. Nor is it entirely fiction. The cases that Audrey and Ryan work on are all taken from real-life circumstances that have been fictionalized.

And now Ryan has a message for you. "Hi, I'm Ryan. I'm on my way to sleep off a thirty-six-hour run and just wanted to say that I have a feeling you aren't going to want to put this book down so be sure the stove isn't on, the kids are safe and work is done for the day. And if you live alone and don't have a dog–get one."

I love to hear from my readers! You can visit me at www.tarataylorquinn.com; e-mail me at ttquinn@tarataylorquinn.com. Or write to me at P.O. Box 13584, Mesa, AZ 85216.

Happy reading!

Tara Taylor Quinn

Tara Taylor Quinn
Trusting Ryan

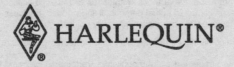

HARLEQUIN®

TORONTO • NEW YORK • LONDON
AMSTERDAM • PARIS • SYDNEY • HAMBURG
STOCKHOLM • ATHENS • TOKYO • MILAN • MADRID
PRAGUE • WARSAW • BUDAPEST • AUCKLAND

ISBN-13: 978-0-373-71500-8
ISBN-10:   0-373-71500-5

TRUSTING RYAN

www.eHarlequin.com

Printed in U.S.A.

ABOUT THE AUTHOR

With more than forty-five original novels, published in more than twenty languages, Tara Taylor Quinn is a *USA TODAY* bestselling author. She is known for delivering deeply emotional and psychologically astute novels. Ms. Quinn is a three-time finalist for the RWA RITA® Award, a multiple finalist for the National Reader's Choice Award, the Reviewer's Choice Award, the Bookseller's Best Award and the Holt Medallion. Ms. Quinn recently married her college sweetheart and the couple currently lives in Ohio with their two very demanding and spoiled bosses: four-pound Taylor Marie and fifteen-pound rescue mutt/cockapoo, Jerry. When she's not writing for Harlequin and MIRA Books or fulfilling speaking engagements, Ms. Quinn loves to travel with her husband, stopping wherever the spirit takes them. They've been spotted in casinos and quaint little antique shops all across the country.

Books by Tara Taylor Quinn

To Tim,
my own young hero who's all grown up now.
I love you more today than yesterday.

CHAPTER ONE

THE WOMAN WAS too damned gorgeous for his good. When he was with her, he couldn't focus on anything else. Including the reasons why he, Columbus Police Detective Ryan Mercedes—one of the city's youngest and newest special victim detectives—was not going to get romantically involved with anyone anytime in the near future.

Most particularly, he was mesmerized by her laughter—had been since he'd first met her six months before at the adoption of an incest victim he'd rescued. The young girl had been Audrey's client.

"What?" Audrey Lincoln asked, glancing over at him in the small living room of his one-bedroom loft condominium.

On the TV Bruce—Jim Carrey—had just been endowed with God's powers and had single-handedly taken on the gang of thugs who'd earlier beaten him up. The scene involved a birth-worthy monkey and cracked Ryan up every time he saw it.

"Nothing," he said, maintaining eye contact with the woman sitting next to him. They'd started hanging out a few months ago. Catching an occasional movie or meeting for a cup of coffee.

"I thought you liked this movie."

Bruce Almighty. He'd seen it so many times the lines randomly popped into his head. "I do."

"You said it was your favorite."

"It is."

"Then why aren't you watching it?"

Good question.

"I am."

Her brown eyes narrowed in a way that made him hungry. She stared at him a second longer, then turned back to the large screen television across from them.

They weren't dating. Weren't on a date. They were just friends. Watching a movie on a Saturday night.

So what if, the week before, they'd moved their watching from a generic theater to his home?

This was where the old movies were.

They'd watched her favorite movie, *The Mirror Has Two Faces,* the previous week. She'd said she related to the main character, Barbra Streisand's version of a university sociology professor. The woman had struggled with being ugly. Undesirable.

Audrey Lincoln had no such worries.

"What?" She was looking at him again.

Sorry, Jim, Ryan silently apologized to the actor who'd given him more hours of hilarious entertainment mixed with just a bit of life lesson than he could count. "You thirsty?" he asked his guest.

"A little."

He stood. Delilah, the cat, opened one eye from her perch on the back of the recliner. "Wine, beer or diet soda?"

"A glass of wine would be great."

He thought so, too. It meant she'd have to stay around a while. Or he'd be forced to arrest her for DUI, and they certainly couldn't have that.

AUDREY COULDN'T remember ever laughing so hard. And she'd seen most of Jim Carrey's movies more than once. Was familiar with his brand of humor. Enjoyed it. Just never this much.

Or perhaps—she glanced over at the handsome detective sitting on the other end of the couch finishing off his glass of wine—it was the company?

Credits rolled. She didn't want the evening to end. Tomorrow it was back to work—no matter that the calendar read Sunday. Audrey hadn't had a day off in longer than she could remember.

She didn't really want one.

Days off led to introspection, which led to...

Nothing that she needed to be concerned about tonight.

"Okay, so tell me why that's your favorite movie," she said, smiling at her companion.

He shrugged, leaving the remote on the table beside him, the DVD flashing its welcome screen. "It's funny."

"And?"

"How do you know there's more?" His glance was intense again—just as it had been during the movie. Her stomach tightened, whether from reaction or dread, she wasn't sure.

Maybe both.

For a thirty-five-year-old woman who spent her days trying to protect the hearts of damaged children, she was embarrassingly inexperienced when it came to matters of her own heart.

"I may have known you only a few months, Mercedes,

but for a cop who's been around long enough to make detective, you're surprisingly empathetic. That's an amazing feat. One that only a man with some depth could manage. So, show me the depth. Why's that your favorite movie?"

The wine was talking. Ordinarily, Audrey would never be so bold. Especially not with a man she actually liked. More than as just an acquaintance. A peer.

Were they actually becoming friends?

She couldn't remember the last time she'd had a personal friend.

"I don't know." Ryan didn't look away as many men would have when faced with a touchy-feely question. "Maybe because I'm a control freak and the idea of having God's power is so compelling I have to keep coming back for more?"

She studied him. Thought about what he said. Shook her head. "I don't think so."

"Why not?"

"Because you aren't power-hungry."

"How do you know?"

"You let me handle the Markovich kid."

"You're his guardian ad litem. He knows you. Trusts you."

"And you were the arresting officer. Jurisdiction was yours. Most cops I know would not have stepped back."

"I still arrested him."

"You took him to the station to keep him safe."

"I charged him."

"He beat up his stepfather. He had to know there were consequences for that."

Scott Markovich was safe now. For now. He was one of her "jobs" for tomorrow. She was making a visit to the fifteen-year-old in detention.

"How do you do it?" Ryan's gaze was piercing. Personal.

A combination that was dangerous to her budding sense of awareness around him. The tight jeans he was wearing and close-fitting polo shirt, stretching across the breadth of his shoulders, didn't help.

Or maybe it was just that she'd always been a sucker for light hair and green eyes.

"How do I do what?" She wanted a little more wine, but didn't want to be too forward.

And she needed to go. Get home to her house. To her nice big pillow-top mattress and down pillows and lose herself in rejuvenating oblivion for a few hours so that she could get up tomorrow and start all over again.

"How do you see all the stuff you do—kids like Markovich who've been sexually abused by people in positions of authority over them—and be able to get close to them? To suffer with them? How do you even get up in the morning, knowing that's what you're going to face?"

How could she not? was the better question.

"How do you?"

"I don't get close. I see them for a few minutes and my job is done. And I'm not always dealing with the little ones. I work with adult victims, too." The room's dim light cast shadows over his frown.

"Still, *why* do you do what you do? Face danger every day—dealing with the toughest to handle crimes."

He seemed to give her question serious consideration. "I don't have a good answer for you. I've wanted to be a cop since I was a kid, never asked myself why. I just know that if I can make a difference, I have to try."

There was more to his story. Audrey didn't succeed at her

job without being able to read between the lines, to read people, to hear what they weren't saying as much or more than what they were. And she didn't succeed without knowing when not to push.

Ryan Mercedes was a private man. An intriguing man. A man who had the looks of Adonis and the heart of Cupid.

A man who was occupying her thoughts so often he was making her uncomfortable.

"How about you?" he asked. "*Why* do you do the work you do?"

For maybe the first time ever, she considered telling someone the whole truth. *Considered.*

"In 2003, in Ohio alone, there were 47,444 substantiated cases of child abuse and or neglect. More than seven thousand of them required the services of a guardian ad litem." Hide behind the facts. It had always been her way. People couldn't argue with facts. And win.

"I understand the need for child advocates," Ryan said. "Remember, I see the results of child abuse and know full well that there are far too many children in this city who need someone on their side, someone looking out only for them and their best interests. But that's not what I asked. I asked, why you?"

His perception surprised her. Or maybe not. Maybe her heart already knew that this man was good for her. That he was personal. In a life that was anything but.

She opened her mouth to tell him about the volunteer guardian ad litem program. The hours of training it took for one qualified ad litem to emerge. The need for legal advocates sitting alongside children in court to help clear up the confusion that stole childhoods.

And about the few of them, the paid lawyer ad litems

who, in addition to looking out for the child's best interests and supporting the child, also offered legal advocacy.

She opened her mouth and said, "I...had a...rough childhood." And in spite of the heat in her cheeks, the discomfort attacking her from the inside out, she couldn't seem to stop. "Other than my parents' divorce, things looked fine on the surface. Middle-class, well-dressed mom with a college education and respectable job. No one could see the things that went on underneath the surface, behind the closed doors of our home. And trying to get anyone to listen, when things looked so picture perfect, proved impossible."

His frown deepened. "She hit you?" He sounded as though he'd like to hit her mother back, and Audrey almost smiled. Too many years had passed, the wounds had healed, and still it felt good to have someone come to her rescue.

She was falling for this man.

"No," she said. "She suffers from depression, though she refused counseling and has never been treated. Sometimes she's fine, but when the darkness descends, watch out. She'll turn on me without warning. Her way of loving is to control. If you do something to displease her, she'll take away her love. And anything else she's providing that she knows you want."

"Such as?"

"When I turned sixteen, she gave me a car. I needed it to get to the university where I was attending class as part of a special high-school-student program. From that point on, she used that car to control me. From the classes I took, the people I chose as friends, the jobs I applied for, the clothes I wore, the church I attended, even the boys I dated. If I didn't do as she suggested, she'd take away my car. Or my college-tuition money. Or the roof over my head. She'd tell me what to think, how to act, who to love. She used to write these horrible letters, telling me how stupid I was, how I never *came to the table,* as she called it, or that I came late. Anytime anything went wrong, it was because I'd screwed up again."

"Where was your dad through all of this?"

"I'm not sure. They divorced before I was a year old. Mom told him he wasn't my real father, but there's never been anyone else in her life that I'm aware of."

"You didn't get tested, to find out if the man was your father?"

Audrey kept thinking that she'd stop the conversation. Right after the next sentence.

But something about Detective Ryan Mercedes compelled her to talk to him. She'd never met anyone like him. Such a mixture of idealism and rigid determination. He was a man you could count on to protect the tribe. But one with a heart, as well.

"He wasn't interested in proving anything," she said.

"Did you ever see him?"

"Nope. I don't even know what he looks like. I wrote to him once, when I was in high school, but the letter came back with a big 'return to sender' on the front. My mother said it was his handwriting."

"And she never told you who your father really was?"

It did sound rather fantastic, now that she heard her story aloud. Audrey was so used to that part of her circumstances, it seemed normal to her. And in her line of work, representing children whose rights were in jeopardy, she regularly saw familial situations that were much more dysfunctional than hers had ever been.

"I've always assumed that the man listed on my birth

certificate, the man she was married to, was my father. My mother has a way of changing the truth to suit her in the moment. She uses words to lash out and hurt when she's hurting, but I don't think she'd have been unfaithful to her marriage vows."

"He must have known that."

"Probably. But she uses people's vulnerabilities against them until she breaks them down to the point where they'll agree with her just to get some peace. I'm guessing she hit him where it counts one too many times."

Audrey sat forward. She'd said too much. Far too much.

"Nice guy, to leave his kid all alone with that woman."

"He paid child support, every single month, until I turned eighteen."

"Like money was going to make you happy? Protect you?"

Life was black and white to Ryan. There was right and wrong. Good and bad. You chose the right. Righted the wrongs. Served good and obliterated the bad.

A characteristic that had drawn her to him from the beginning. The world needed more of his kind of passion.

She just didn't want to need it. Not on a personal level.

"Maybe he thought, since I was a girl, her daughter, that there'd be some kind of motherly instinct that would come out in her, protect me from the emotional abuse he must have suffered."

"Or maybe he sucked as a father."

Ryan's words made her smile.

"YOU NEVER DID answer my question." Ryan wished he'd brought the wine bottle in with him. Wished he could pour another glass for both of them. Keep her on his couch with him.

At least for a time.

Long enough to get to know her well enough to get her out of his system. To dispel the strange and uncomfortable hold she had on him.

Ryan was used to being his own man. He'd been hearing the beat of his own drummer for most of his life. And walked to it alone.

He liked it that way.

He had things to do with his life—lives to save and evils to conquer—and he couldn't do that if he gave his heart away.

Or at least that was the story he'd been telling himself. If there was another reason, some deep-seated something that prevented him from living the normal life of wife and kids and family, he didn't want to know about it.

"What question?" Her big brown eyes were mysterious, pulling him into their shadowed depths, as she flung a lock of her long blond hair over her shoulder. She sat on the edge of the couch, as though poised for flight. He wished she'd relax again.

"Why you do what you do."

"Oh, I thought I had. That's easy. I spent my childhood feeling powerless," she said as though that explained it all.

And in a sense, it did. She'd been stripped of something vital as a child. And every day, when she went to work, when her work preserved the dignity and sense of self of even one child, when she protected the innocence of childhood, she took back the personal power she'd lost.

Ryan understood that. Righting wrongs was what made his past, his history, his genealogy conscionable, too.

CHAPTER TWO

AUDREY DIDN'T WAIT around for his call. And only checked her cell phone so many times Sunday evening because she gave the number to all her clients, and if a child needed her, tomorrow could be too late.

It wasn't Ryan's fault she'd bared her soul like an idiot the night before. He had no way of knowing she'd shared with him more than she'd ever told anyone.

She'd come across like some pathetic victim, instead of the strong and healthy woman she'd become.

With the hundred-year-old hardwood floors of her Victorian-style cottage shining, she put away the cleaning supplies she'd hauled out and went upstairs to the treadmill. And half an hour later, panting and sweaty, headed across the hall to her home office—the only other room upstairs—and read over her files for the next day.

When everyone else in the world was relaxing, watching television, reading, napping, Audrey worked.

The kids whose lives seemed reduced to files of unfortunate facts, whose parents, for a variety of reasons, were unable to parent effectively, called out to her. They were always calling out to her.

Kaylee Grady. Date of birth, 9/29/04. That made her four years old. Audrey looked through the documents of the new case she had an initial meeting on the following morning.

Kelsey Grady. Date of birth, 9/29/04.

Twins.

Lifting the cover page, she studied the picture underneath. They were identical. Blond. With chubby cheeks—and far too serious eyes. Their parents had been killed in a car accident during a blizzard the previous February. There'd been no will. And the family was fighting over custody. They wanted to split up the girls to satisfy members from both sides.

"Over my dead body." Audrey's voice, usually a comfort, sounded loud in the gabled room. Loud and lonely.

And she glanced at the cell phone she'd carried up with her. Nothing. No missed calls. No messages.

She didn't blame him for not calling.

The cuckoo clock in the family room downstairs of her 1920s, whitewashed home chirped eight times. Not meaning to, Audrey counted every one, and then knew what time it was. A piece of information she'd purposely been denying herself.

It was just that, last night, she and Ryan had crossed into new territory. Hadn't they?

That of friends, trusted friends. Or something. It wasn't as though they were kids, playing the dating game. They were mature adults. Getting to know each other. Sharing a moment in time.

A phone call would have been nice. That was all.

HE WAS STILL WORKING the eleven-to-seven shift. Not because he had to—no, Ryan Mercedes had all the right contacts in all the right places, whether he wanted them or not. He was on the night shift for one reason only.

A selfish reason.

Working nights allowed him to keep his distance from everyone in his life. Having to sleep when family gatherings happened, when an old school mate suggested going out for beers, anytime he was issued an invitation that got a little bit too close, he could always bow out with the excuse that he was working.

The night shift let him operate in a different world. A world where everyone slept—except those few who were working as well, or those who took advantage of others' sleep to commit crimes against them.

The downside was, when he came off shift Monday morning, he was completely exhausted and wired at the same time. He'd been awake all day Sunday having dinner with his birth parents—he hadn't seen two-month-old Marcus Ryan in over a week, and his biological cousin, Jordon, a fatherless young man Ryan had met the previous summer who seemed to gravitate to him, had been visiting from Cleveland. Then he'd visited his adoptive parents to watch the Reds game on television with his dad.

He hadn't been to bed since Saturday night. And that session hadn't contained his most restful sleep with the continuous interruptions of vivid dreams of a certain lady in the bed with him.

He'd never had a woman in his bed at the condo. Never had a woman in his bed, period.

So why was one suddenly appearing there, uninvited?

He wanted to think she was unwanted, but his body wouldn't let him go quite that far.

He settled for…uninvited.

And still, nearly thirty-six hours after she'd left his apartment, he was thinking about her.

He was on shift again that night, Ryan reminded himself as he drove slowly through the streets of Westerville, cell phone in hand. Two kids were waiting for the school bus on the corner of Cleveland Avenue and Homeacres Drive. Usually there were three. The shorter girl was missing.

Ryan made a mental note to take the same route home tomorrow. And the next day. If the girl was still missing by the end of the week, he'd stop and ask about her.

In the meantime, he had to sleep. And sleep well. He couldn't do his job on adrenaline alone. His instincts wouldn't be as sharp. Lives could be at risk.

He had to get some rest.

"Hello?"

Her number was on speed dial only because a couple of her clients were under his investigation.

"Audrey? Is this a bad time? Did I wake you?"

Seven-thirty in the morning was early to some people.

"Of course not. I've been up a couple of hours."

Well, then… "Are you at work? With someone? Should I call another time?"

"No, Ryan." She chuckled. "This time is fine. I don't have to be in court until ten-thirty this morning, and my breakfast meeting canceled."

Canceled. She was free for breakfast. Unexpectedly. The thought of asking her to meet him somewhere for a quick bite sent alarm signals up his spine. Where was the harm in two friends having breakfast?

They both had to eat.

"So what's up?" she asked, bringing to his attention the length of time he'd let lapse while he blubbered over the idea of asking her out to eat.

Shifting in his seat, adjusting the pistol digging into his thigh beneath the brown tweed sports jacket he wore, Ryan thought about the case he'd been working on for most of the night.

Focused on the life he'd chosen to live.

The juvenile who'd beaten his stepfather to a pulp, claiming that it was self-defense. He'd claimed some other pretty horrendous things, too.

Reviewing four hours of witness testimony, tapes, doctors' reports and police records had netted Ryan no more than they already had.

"The prosecutor's going to charge Markovich."

"No way." He heard the drop in her voice and felt as if he'd failed not only the fifteen-year-old boy whom he'd believed, but Audrey, too.

"The kid's testimony has too many holes," he said. "He contradicts himself on four separate occasions."

"But there's a doctor's report that proves he was molested."

"At some point in his life. Not necessarily by his stepfather."

"He nearly killed the man, Ryan. A fifteen-year-old kid, especially one as sensitive as Scott, doesn't suddenly get violent unless something pretty vile is going to happen to him."

"I know." He was missing something. He just didn't know what. "But it's not my job to be the lawyer," he reminded himself as much as her. "I check out the facts, make the arrests, collect the evidence, then I'm done."

"You aren't, though, are you?" The soft question surprised him.

And then it didn't. He'd called her, hadn't he?

"No," he admitted. "The kid's lying about something, but not about why he unhinged on his stepfather, I'm sure of it. Unless I can find out what else is going on, the kid's going back to detention. Maybe for a long, long time."

"They aren't charging him as an adult, are they?"

Ryan wasn't sure. But he'd heard a rumor that they might. He let his silence answer for him.

And because he'd called to escape the sometimes hell of his job, he asked another question that had been plaguing him on and off for more than a week.

"Why do you relate so much to *The Mirror Has Two Faces?*"

The woman was gorgeous. Not only the classic beauty of long blonde hair, long legs, great figure and big brown eyes, but also the sensitivity that shone through those eyes, especially in one so young, the job she'd chosen to do when, with her law degree, she could be making a mint, made her irresistible.

As a friend only, of course.

"I don't know."

It was one of *those* "I don't know"s. The kind that really meant, "I don't want to tell you."

"I think you do."

"Maybe."

"So tell me."

Another long pause.

"I told you why I like *Bruce Almighty.*"

"Because you have power envy."

The more commonly used *p*-word in that phrase sprang immediately to mind, and Ryan was grateful that Audrey couldn't read his thoughts.

Glad, too, that they were on the phone and not where she could see the reaction hearing her voice was having on that *p* part of his anatomy.

Turning, he pulled into the parking lot of his complex. Parked in the covered lot and headed around to his door. His place was only a one-bedroom, but it was two stories with a private patio that looked out over a golf course.

"So why do you?" Delilah, the cat he had because he was gone too much to have a dog, wrapped herself around his legs as he let himself in and dropped his keys on the table by the front door.

"Why do I have power envy?" she asked, the amusement in her voice sending another surge of blood beneath his fly.

With Delilah under one arm, like the football he'd never carried in high school, Ryan entered the kitchen, looking for the opened can of tuna in the fridge.

"Why do you relate to *The Mirror Has Two Faces?*"

"You're like a dog with a bone, you know that?"

"Yeah."

"Don't you ever get sidetracked?"

"Not often."

Delilah munched from the can. Ryan snagged a chunk of the white fishy meat, dropped it in a bowl and looked for the mayonnaise. Not bacon and eggs, but it would do.

"I'm waiting," he said.

"What are you doing?"

"Eating."

"Eating what?"

"I'm not telling you until you tell me why you identify with that movie."

"Fine." The word was clipped, but her tone wasn't nearly

aggrieved enough to convey any real irritation. "I've always thought that kind of relationship would be perfect."

"What kind? The kind where they end up dancing in the street?"

"No." Her voice had quieted. Lost the playfulness. "I'd love to have a best friend, a significant other, someone to come home to, without messing everything up with sex."

Not what he'd expected to hear. Where was his opportunity to tell her that she was gorgeous? That she had no reason to think herself anything but beautiful? It was all about what you saw in the mirror, right? The way you see yourself, as opposed to how others see you.

"So get a roommate."

"Roommates leave. Get married. I want a lifetime companion."

He couldn't believe she meant that. "A sexless one." Hell, everyone knew that part of the movie was crazy. Even the stars of the movie found that out.

It didn't work. *Couldn't* work. Unless maybe one of the parties was gay...

"At least one where the relationship isn't based on sex," she said slowly, as though choosing her words with great care. "If, after we've lived together for a while, we decide we want to do that some time, that would be fine. As long as we both want it. And it isn't a big deal one way or the other."

The woman was nuts. Sex, not a big deal? She couldn't really expect any guy with blood in his veins to live with someone as beautiful as she was and not burn up with a need to make love with her. Could she?

"So you'd do it once?" he asked, out of morbid curiosity. "Or do it once in a while?"

"I don't know." She drew the statement out. "That's the whole point. Whether we ever did it or not wouldn't matter. If we both wanted to, we could. If one of us didn't want to, no big deal. The relationship would be based on mutual respect. Trust. Great conversation. Just enjoying being together."

If one of us didn't want to. Alarms went off in Ryan's head. The kind he'd honed to perfection.

"Are you gay?"

The question was inappropriate. Disrespectful. Uncalled for. And not what he'd really wanted to ask at all. He just didn't know how to find out what he suddenly needed to know.

"No. But that's a typical guy response."

"I'm a guy."

But not a typical one.

"I'm not gay."

"But you've been abused, haven't you?" He wasn't pleased with himself, with the words. His tone had lowered enough that maybe she hadn't heard him.

"If you're asking if I was raped, the answer's no."

Thank God. Thank God in heaven. Shocked at the emotion pricking at the back of his throat, his eyelids, Ryan grabbed a carton of juice from the refrigerator and took a huge swallow.

"But you've been in a relationship where you had sex because you felt like you had to."

"That's kind of a personal question, don't you think?"

"Yeah."

"Well, I told you why I liked the movie. Now I want to know what you're having for breakfast."

Fair enough. But he figured they both knew she wasn't getting off the hook permanently. "Tuna."

"You made a sandwich?"

"No. Just tuna."

"With dressing?"

"Nope. Couldn't find any."

"You're eating tuna out of the can."

"Ate. It's gone." Thanks to Delilah. She wasn't great at sharing.

"And that's all you're going to have?"

"I'm on my way to bed," he reminded her, trying not to remember the images of her that he'd taken to his repose the last time he'd been there.

"What time do you get up?"

"Depends on the day."

"Today."

"I'm planning to crash until I wake up. No alarms. Which means I'll probably make it until around three." If he was lucky.

If not, he'd be up in an hour. Even with room-darkening curtains he couldn't lie in bed during the day if he was awake. There was always someone to see, or talk to, who wasn't available in the middle of the night.

Like the cable company that was supposed to be adding Sportzone to his monthly service—had charged him, but failed to turn on the games.

"You think you'll want some breakfast then?"

"I'm sure I will." If you could call stale bread and peanut butter breakfast. He hadn't been to the grocery store. Saturday nights were usually reserved for that because it was the only time of the week the place wasn't milling with people.

"I make a mean omelet."

Ryan's blood started to pump harder again, all signs of exhaustion taking a hike. Had she just invited him to her place?

"I'm glad to hear that."

"I have a seven-o'clock meeting tonight, but nothing after court this afternoon. If you'd like to stop by, I could show you my ham-and-cheese."

"Okay." Sure. He crossed one scuffed wing-tipped shoe over the other. Nonchalance was called for.

He just had to find some.

"If you want to, that is," she added in a bit of a rush. "I mean, you've provided dinner the past two Saturday nights. I thought I should return the favor."

He'd ordered pizza.

"That'd be great," he said with a tight rein on himself. *Don't make anything out of it, Mercedes. The woman's beautiful. And not interested in sex. Or you. Or she'd be interested in sex.*

And he wasn't interested, either. His obsession with her was a blip. Like the flu.

"It's not a big deal," she said. "I mean, I'm just offering one friend to another."

"Hey, Audrey." He added a teasing chuckle to his tone— he hoped. "It's fine. I'm a bachelor. I never say no to home-made food. No strings attached."

"Good. Fine." The confidence had returned to her voice. "Say, around five, then?"

Five was fine. That left him seven and a half hours to get his libido under control and forget that he'd ever had one intimate thought about a stunningly desirable guardian ad litem.

He was not the least bit interested in a long term relationship.

And one thing was certain. Audrey Lincoln was not a woman a good man had casual sex with. She was the type of woman he loved.

CHAPTER THREE

THE OMELET didn't happen. The phone rang, instead, and Audrey only had time to scramble some eggs and take five minutes to eat them with Ryan before running off to be at Mollie Anderson's mother's house when the confused twelve-year-old's father came to pick her up for visitation.

Neither of Mollie's parents had known she was coming because Mollie had been the one to call for Audrey's help.

Audrey talked to Ryan again on Wednesday morning. He phoned as he came off his shift to ask her about another case they'd shared—a pair of nine-year-old fraternal twins who'd initially been reported as runaways several months before. Very soon into the investigation, however, they'd realized the twins had been abducted.

Ryan thought he might have located them living in Arizona with a man who, other than the color and length of his hair, perfectly fit the description of the children's father.

She'd grieved for Darla and Danny Buford for months until she'd finally, with the help of some counseling, let them go. There'd been an obvious break-in at Mrs. Buford's well-to-do home. A ransom note.

Mr. Buford, the other half of the lengthy and ugly divorce that initially had brought Audrey into the picture, had been right beside his ex-wife through the entire ordeal. He'd paid half the ransom and cried with his ex-wife in his arms when the terms of the bargain were not met.

The money disappeared. The police didn't catch the slight figure who'd picked up the bag in the middle of the busy New York City street where the kids supposedly had been taken. And the children were never returned.

The kids were dead. Plain and simple.

And shockingly, horribly, grossly unfair.

Audrey wanted Ryan to be right about the Arizona lead, but she didn't think so.

Yet that didn't stop her from hoping. If any other detective had told her he'd located those kids, she'd have shrugged off the news without much thought. But Ryan Mercedes's track record for accuracy was impressive.

Because he didn't speak until he knew what he was saying? Or because he was that gifted at his job?

He called again on Friday morning. The Buford twins were alive.

"Turns out some psycho, who'd just lost his wife and daughter in a car accident, had taken them. He never let them out of his sight."

"What about school?" Audrey prided herself on the professional tone—glad that Ryan couldn't see the moisture in her eyes.

"He home-schooled them. They're pretty confused, but physically unharmed. The state has them until their parents can get there."

Audrey had to take a deep breath to let the emotion pass. There were so many more tragic stories in her line of work than happy endings. "Mr. and Mrs. Buford are going together?"

"They remarried more than a month ago."

Thankful that at least two traumatized children had every advantage for full recovery, Audrey listened as Ryan offered to grill a steak for her that night to celebrate a homecoming they both took personally, yet neither would attend.

"I can't." It was for the best, she told the part of herself that was disappointed. "I'm having dinner with a therapist who had a session with one of my clients yesterday."

Both she and the therapist were booked for the next week, but Audrey wasn't willing to settle for a paper report on this one. Nor could she wait a week. The family was due in court again on Monday.

Saturday night she had a fund-raiser with the Arizona Bar Association, and on Sunday she was volunteering legal services at a women's shelter.

All things she did because she loved to do them. Wanted to do them. Because they gave her life meaning. And a reason to get up in the morning.

The activities were designed to create the life she wanted. And that was exactly what she had as she hung up the phone, fully aware that Ryan thought she'd been making excuses not to see him again. Fully aware that she might never hear from him again—outside the office.

Fully aware and completely okay.

It was very unsettling, therefore, that a time or two over the weekend she almost resented those same activities. Mostly when she was thinking of the handsome detective and wondering what he was doing with his two days off, living in real-world time.

Still, a little resentment, in exchange for the ability to live her own life, was a small price to pay.

When her phone rang again Monday morning at the time

Ryan was due off shift, she picked it up with far too much vigor. And flooded with warmth when she heard his voice.

Get a grip, my girl, she admonished herself. *He's a friend. Nothing more.*

"Do you have any free time this week?" he asked after a brief hello. He sounded as impatient as she felt over the past weekend's misses. Not angry. More like…needy.

Or maybe she was projecting her own eagerness onto him?

"I have a couple of hours between court hearings tomorrow, starting around eleven, but you're sleeping then," she told him.

"I'll stay up."

"What—and get yourself killed tomorrow night?"

"I can sleep after lunch."

"Are we having lunch?"

"I think so."

"Okay."

AND THEY DID. She had a quick dinner with him on Thursday, too, before her guest lecture at the Moritz College of Law at Ohio State. They talked about work. About the weather and the Cincinnati Reds and about work some more.

She asked about Delilah.

They didn't talk about each other. And the more they didn't, the more Audrey wanted to.

What was the matter with her?

She'd never needed a man to complete her before. To the contrary, she did better, felt stronger and more capable, when she wasn't with a man.

So why couldn't she stop looking at him? Whether he was

wearing jeans and a T-shirt, exhausted and on his way to sleep, or wearing a jacket on his way to work, the man looked like an art sculpture to her. Legs that were long and lean and nothing but delineated muscle, shoulders that blocked the clouds from her view when he stood in front of her, eyes that smiled, or admired, or sympathized without guise, and a butt that—

No. She wasn't going to think about that. Wasn't going to think that way. She wanted a friendship.

She didn't want sex. Didn't want to be that vulnerable. A man might be able to join his body parts with a woman, share pleasure with her, and get dressed and walk away, but not Audrey. Nope, she'd open her heart right along with her legs, then she'd be right back where she'd been at sixteen. Craving love. Needing validation from someone who could give it, or take it away, without notice.

No butt looked good enough to risk that.

RYAN STAYED UP on Friday after work. He had two days off, plans to see Marcus Ryan—because he couldn't seem to stay away from the baby recently born to the biological parents he'd met the previous year—to go to a Reds game with the dad who'd raised him, and have some of his mom's home cooking. He needed to be on the same time as the rest of the world.

He also needed to shop and clean his place before Audrey showed up at six expecting steaks on a grill he didn't yet have. He didn't have the food, either, or furniture for the patio, but those were minor details.

Things to take his mind off the rape victim he'd watched being loaded into an ambulance at three that morning. What

in the hell a middle-aged married woman had been doing out
in a deserted school parking lot by herself in the middle of
the night, he didn't know.

But he hoped to God she lived to tell him. One way or
another, as the newest detective in the Special Victims Unit,
he was going to find out.

His place was ready, new furniture assembled, grill put
together, salad made and steaks marinated by five. Up in the
master-suite loft, Ryan showered, pulled on some jeans and
a black T-shirt, ran his fingers through his hair—then
decided to shave again. Just for something to do.

Ten minutes later he still had forty minutes to kill.
Avoiding the king-size bed, avoiding thoughts of his dinner
guest in that bed, he checked his cell phone for messages.

Nothing from work. Good. Sometimes it was nice not
to be needed.

Needed. He adjusted his jeans. Ryan wanted to be
needed. Bad.

He needed his watch.

Walking around the massive bed to the nightstand where
he'd left the timepiece his father had given him when he'd
made detective—it had a tiny recording device built into it—
Ryan glanced at the comforter.

It was clean. The browns and beiges were kind of masculine, but then, he was a guy. Guys tended to be masculine.

The sheets were light-colored. While he tried to see them
from a woman's perspective, a thought occurred to him. He
hadn't changed them in a while.

Never seemed to have the time.

He had twenty minutes right now.

Only because he so rarely had extra time, only because

he needed to take advantage of that time to accomplish something, Ryan changed his sheets.

He'd just finished when the doorbell rang.

HE'D SEEN HER in jeans before. Several times. Just didn't remember them fitting those long, feminine thighs quite so well. The white, short-sleeved T-shirt covered the waistband. As long as she didn't move.

"Wine?" he asked, handing her a glass as she sat in the wicker rocker he'd purchased that afternoon.

She lifted her hand to take the glass. "Thanks." Ryan had to turn away before she noticed his reaction to the thin strip of lightly tanned stomach she'd exposed.

He'd have raised his gaze to avoid that possibility, except that her breasts, which were round and full and completely framed by the tight shirt, were far too much temptation.

He was a solitary man. With a job to do. People to protect.

Maybe he should go next door. That way he wouldn't see her. Wouldn't flirt with temptation. He could cook on his neighbor's grill and courier the steaks over....

"I talked to Scott Markovich today."

The kid who'd beat up his stepdad. The bastard dad was going to live. Thank God. As it stood, Scott had been charged with assault, which was a lot better than murder.

And talking about work was a lot better than...anything else.

"And?"

"I think he's protecting his mother."

"She was out of town when the incident took place."

Audrey's hair fell forward across her shoulder as she shook her head.

"I don't think so. I think she was there. I think she'd been drinking again."

"I thought the court ordered that she'd lose custody of Scott if she went back on the juice."

"Right."

Realization dawned and Ryan blurted, "She knows what happened that night."

"I think so."

"And she won't speak up because she was drunk."

Audrey shrugged.

"She knows what that SOB was going to do to her son."

"That's my guess."

Ryan swore, his mind racing ahead—and back at the same time. Going over the reports he'd practically memorized, looking for clues he'd missed. Trying to figure out how he was going to prove Audrey's theory.

"Her sister wasn't her only alibi. There was the bus driver who took her to Detroit," he reminded her.

And maybe the guy was dating the sister. Or had lied for favors. Maybe he'd been drinking on the job and couldn't remember who he'd transported and had lied to save his ass.

Maybe...

"There was the woman who sold her the ticket, too," she added.

Didn't mean she got on the bus. "No passengers remembered her."

"It was the middle of the night," Audrey said, not that he hadn't already been thinking the same thing himself.

"There were only two of them and they were both asleep," he finished for her.

The evidence was mostly circumstantial. But Scott had openly threatened to kill his stepdad the previous year. And there was no denying that the kid had used the crowbar on the man's back. The only question was why.

"If we can get it on the record that she was there that night, we can subpoena her to testify. If her husband had been about to rape her son, any halfway-decent attorney should be able to get a self-defense dismissal out of that."

Her eyes had the fire of battle, the glow of an imminent win, and Ryan was almost a little sad that she'd opted not to practice law. She'd make a damned good prosecutor. And Lord knew the world needed them.

But she was young. Fresh out of law school, he figured, based on the fact that she'd taken the bar exam the previous year. There was time.

"As strongly as I believe you," he said, sitting down beside her, wishing he'd opted for the footed double swing rather than two chairs, "I can't put theory on report."

"I think I can get Scott to talk to you, if you're willing."

Sitting forward, Ryan almost spilled his drink. "Hell, yes, I'm willing."

"It'll have to be tomorrow. They're moving him to a facility in Dayton until his trial. Something about bed space in the non-sexual-offense unit for fifteen-year-olds."

"Fine."

The Reds game might have to wait. His dad would understand.

SHE'D HAD BETTER steak. Apparently Ryan liked them very well-done. But Audrey couldn't remember anyone whose company she'd enjoyed more.

"I like how you think," she told him, trying not to over-react as he sat next to her on the darkened patio, handing her the half-glass of wine she'd requested.

His eyes, as they stared at her, glistened with two white spots, a double reflection of the moon shining overhead. "You like how I think? What does that mean?"

"I don't know." She should go. Before she did something she'd regret. "I like the way your mind works, your take on things. You've got all these theories that are just a bit outside the norm, and yet I agree with them, you know? I like listening to you talk."

And if she didn't shut up she was going to ruin a friendship before it had the chance to exist.

Because her next sentence wasn't going to be about liking his conversation.

"I like how you think, too." The words were offered slowly, softly. A declaration of admiration. At least.

Or so her heart seemed to think. It flip-flopped, sending a sharp blade of desire down through her most feminine places.

Without removing her gaze from his, she took a sip of wine. Moistened a throat that was suddenly far too dry. Inexplicably dry. What was she doing?

Ryan didn't seem to want his wine. Setting down the glass he'd barely touched, he stared at her for a second longer, then leaned forward. Slowly. Deliberating. Coming closer.

She watched, glanced down to his lips, frozen as she waited. There was no thought of action, of shoulds and shouldn'ts, of wants or not wants. No thought of any moment that came before, or any that might come after.

And when those full, masculine lips touched hers, the shiver that went through her wiped away any last conscious thought.

She'd been kissed before. Many times. But never like this.

Ryan's mouth controlled hers, even as it asked permission. He invaded and invited at the same time, taking her on a sensual journey that consumed her entire being with the mere touch of his lips. He was tender. And confident.

And when he pulled back, Audrey couldn't let him go. Her mouth followed his the couple of inches he retreated, until her lips were once again attached to his.

He opened his mouth then, demanding more from her, his tongue finding hers, not just tip to tip, but fully engaging with her in a give-and-take that made them far more intimate than friends.

"I want to make love with you."

She wasn't sure she heard the words at first. Thought maybe she'd imagined them. And even then, her body responded, igniting every nuance of sensual feeling inside of her.

"Please."

There was no mistaking the pleading in his voice.

Or the answering desire inside of her.

Pulling back, Audrey studied those glistening green eyes. "I..."

How did she say no without turning him off? Without losing his interest? What words did she use?

"I want that, too."

She didn't just say that. Didn't just lick her lips. Her nipples weren't hard, sensitive, against her bra.

She couldn't...

Ryan's lips covered hers again, his hands coming up behind her to rest beneath her shoulder blades, pressing her against him, and as she melted into his embrace, Audrey knew that she was going to break her own rules.

CHAPTER FOUR

HE SHOULD HAVE BEEN nervous, for many reasons. Any time he'd thought about this moment in his life—and he'd thought of it plenty over the past ten or so years—Ryan had envisioned shaky hands. Some fumbling. Uncertainty born solely of ignorance.

Hesitation, at the very least, as he risked the isolation he'd so carefully concocted and guarded vigilantly.

Audrey's hands on his shoulders, her moans consuming the air around them, the light flowery scent of her perfume enveloping him, allowed no room for hesitation. Her soft, feminine skin, waiting there for him to find, to expose, to caress, created fire within him, not quivering.

He kissed her, opening her mouth wider with his, exploring her with his tongue in ways that happened naturally, as if of their own accord. With no learned or practiced moves to draw on, he lifted her body gently against him, breaking contact with her lips only briefly, as he carried her to his bed.

He'd be Detective Ryan Mercedes tomorrow. And all of the tomorrows after that.

Tonight he was a man.

He'd made the trek upstairs many times—exhausted and coming off thirty-five hours without sleep, wide awake, early, late, angry, frustrated, enervated, flying up the steps two or three at a time. He'd made it hurt, content, and even drunk once. He'd traversed them alone with a hand truck and solid pine chest of drawers, a bed, his second large-screen television. Tonight he climbed them with no thought of the journey, only of the woman with her arms wrapped around his neck, of getting her to the soft mattress that awaited them so that he could love her properly.

Reverently.

Laying her gently crossways in the middle of the bed, Ryan slid down next to her, covering one of her legs with one of his as he half lay on top of her. He was on fire, needing everything, everywhere, and was compelled to stare at her, instead, to connect, first, through the eyes of her soul, the eyes of her heart and mind, those chocolate-brown windows that gazed back at him with an intensity that matched his own.

"I've wanted this since the first moment I saw you." He confessed what he'd sworn to himself he'd never admit to anyone.

She was his match on a level much deeper than anyone ever had been. But she was independent, too. Surely there was safety in that.

"Have you?" she asked, her voice huskier than usual. The little grin turning up the edges of her mouth made him hard.

Harder.

The bulge in his pants wasn't a new thing. Its control of him was.

"I have," he told her, bending to kiss her again, opening his mouth over hers, needing to get as far inside her as he could, to join as much of him to her as was humanly possible.

And beyond.

Audrey's moan lit another flame in his groin and Ryan

rubbed his aching penis against her denim-clad thigh. He felt like a damned animal, rutting against her.

She didn't seem to mind. Lifting up, Audrey moved back and forth against his chest, pressing her upper body against him until he could clearly distinguish two hard nipples caressing him.

"I like that." He'd had no idea.

"Me, too."

"I'd like to see them." He could only give her honesty.

"Okay."

Her gaze was open, and shadowed with desire, as she studied him. The rest of her didn't move.

Which left him one choice. Glancing down at the rounded mounds of her breasts, he lifted her shirt as though he'd had a lot of experience with such things. With one hand and a smooth glide, the white cotton was bunched up beneath her armpits and the lacy, low-cut bra he'd seen only in outline was fully exposed. The soft skin of her breasts spilled over the edges of the flimsy material.

Heart racing, Ryan took his time, savoring the view. His hands itched to cover those breasts, but he couldn't deny himself the beautiful sight.

"I've never seen anything so perfectly gorgeous." His voice was mostly a whisper. It was all the breath he had to spare.

"You're pretty gorgeous yourself," she said. She'd lifted his T-shirt, as well, was staring at his chest.

She touched him, running slim fingers over the muscles in his chest, stroking her thumbs against his nipples. Flickers of sensation moved through him, straight down to his erection.

His nipples had that kind of power? He'd taken one hell

of a lot of showers, rubbed them with hundreds of bars of soap, to have missed that one.

Mary Ellen Rowe had spent the six weeks they'd dated rubbing his chest. He'd been pleasantly comforted by the touch.

Nothing more.

"That feels good," he told the awesome woman lying in his bed. "Really good."

Her smile was a sweet mixture of knowing and modesty. A woman who was, perhaps, just becoming aware of the depths of her own sexual power, as well?

What the hell was the matter with him? Analyzing, even now. He had breasts waiting before him.

Loving to do.

And still, Ryan couldn't lose his distinct awareness of every single movement, every touch.

These moments were going to be embedded deeply within his memory, his heart, for the rest of his life.

Over the next hour Ryan discovered much about himself. And about Audrey Lincoln. As much focus as she gave to her young clients, she gave to making love with him. Every aspect of her was intent on him. Her gaze. Her touch. Her responses and attention. He'd never felt so consumed—and so alive. She knew him better in an hour than anyone had ever known him.

With fingers skimming the edge of his jeans, she almost drove him over the edge.

He had to release the zipper on his fly. Get his pants off. He had to set his penis free to love a woman. This woman.

Where before he'd moved slowly, savoring, Ryan now pulled at the button of Audrey's pants with more strength than finesse. It came free with one tug. On his knees above her, he bent to her hips, grasping the jeans in both hands to tug them down over slim hips and long legs that seemed to go on and on.

Just when he'd thought it couldn't get any better.

He stared at her thighs. At the scrap of white lace panty that didn't quite cover the dark hair curling there. The thin strap of thong disappearing into her backside.

And something occurred to him.

She'd dressed for this. For him.

Looking up at her, he sought silent confirmation in the gaze that was fully on him.

"You're okay with this." It was more statement than question.

Her lips were trembling as she nodded.

With fingers that were oversensitized, he touched her, the soft skin of her legs, her inner thighs, the brush of hair at the top of her panties. He had to go slowly now, or explode before he ever got where he was going.

"I want yours off, too."

Slow down, Mercedes, he told his raging body as he stood. Unbuttoned his own jeans, stepped out of them— taking his briefs off at the same time.

And then he stood before her, his penis full and weighted down, while she looked at him.

"Okay?" he asked when her gaze finally met his.

Licking her lips, she nodded again.

Ryan was beginning to love that silent affirmation, recognizing that she gave it when she most wanted something.

He meant to take another hour with her, to put his fingers every place he wanted his penis to go, to explore her so thoroughly there would be no part of her unknown to him.

He took a moment to sheath himself with a condom from

the box in his bedside drawer—a supply that he used to replace the one in his wallet each month—and turned back to her.

Taking off her panties as he rejoined her on the bed, he made it only so long as it took him to spread her legs and settle himself between them. He didn't have to wonder what to do. His body knew. He found her opening and gave a slow nudge, his gaze glued to hers.

And he watched her eyes open wider as his penis first penetrated and then, moving gently in and out, filled her more fully.

Nothing had prepared him for the way that felt. *Ecstasy* was too bland a word. *Perfection* not good enough to describe the sensation that filled him from head to toe. Heaven couldn't be this good.

Ryan hadn't known how he'd make certain that Audrey had an orgasm, wasn't sure he'd recognize it when it happened. He only knew that he was not going to take his own pleasure without ensuring hers.

As it turned out, there was no issue. Fully inside her, he pulled out and thrust in again, and again, more quickly, feeling the pressure building in his erection, getting ready to explode, and knowing he was going to have to stop or go before she did when her moans changed, became more frantic, and then surprised-sounding as the inner folds of her body clasped him, pulsing around him. Over and over.

"Oh, my…" Her words were more cry than statement, released breathlessly before she sucked in air.

And with that breath, Ryan joined her, his body erupting with huge throbs as he came inside a woman for the first time in his life.

Highly praised and swiftly rising detective, Ryan Mercedes, had just lost his virginity.

YOU'RE IN TROUBLE, girl. Big trouble.

With Ryan's "Oh, yes," still ringing in her ears, the aftermath of his lovemaking leaving her lethargic and absolutely joyful at the same time, she tried her darnedest to rein herself in. To find reality.

She'd had sex before. Way before. And more recently than that, too. But she'd never made love.

Never felt that liquid heat devour every vein in her body, or known herself to give up control to the wild and free ecstasy he'd built inside her.

It had to be the wine. Or the fact that no one had ever taken more than an hour to have sex with her before.

It had to be how long they'd known each other without acknowledging the attraction between them.

It had to be the overdone steak.

It absolutely could not be that she'd in any way given any part of her heart to the man who was even now inside her.

Making her want to do it again.

"I'm sorry—am I too heavy?" Ryan lifted his shoulder off hers. The chilled air that drifted over her newly exposed skin was not welcome.

"No." With one hand on his backside, holding him in place, and another on his shoulder, she pulled him back down. "You feel good."

"I'm about to fall asleep."

She'd figured so. Any man she'd ever been with—not that there'd been that many—had either jumped up and thrown on clothes immediately afterward, or fallen asleep without a word.

Novel to have someone actually talk to her about doing either.

"Sleep awhile, then," she said softly, thinking she'd do the same herself.

Another first.

"But I don't really want to sleep." He raised up enough to look her in the eye. "I don't want to waste a single moment with you."

Oh, God, I am in serious trouble.

"I think that's just about the sweetest thing anyone has ever said to me." She told her new lover the unadorned truth. And lifted her head to plant a small kiss on lips that were slightly swollen.

Had she done that?

And left that love mark on his neck, too?

Was he going to be angry when he saw that?

Guiding his head gently back down to her chest, she ran her fingers slowly back and forth through his hair. It was full and thick, even for its shortness. And surprisingly soft.

So many things about this man were surprising to her. And yet, not surprising at all. He fit her so exactly, not only where they were still connected, but in all ways. He approached his job as she did, with everything he had, sparing little for any other life. He cared. He didn't give up. He saw reality and still believed.

He had unbounded energy and had found a way, in spite of the experience and time it took to make detective, to avoid cynicism.

The weight of his head grew heavier and she hoped he'd allowed himself to rest. The man had worked all night. And if she had to guess, she'd figure he'd been up all day today, getting ready for tonight.

Everything in the apartment had been perfect. He'd

dusted since she'd been there last. Vacuum marks had still lined the carpet. And the furniture outside was new, added since her previous visit when she'd peeked outside to the empty patio.

Dinner had already been prepared, other than the cooking of the steaks. Even the meat had been marinated.

It all spoke Ryan to her. Attention to every detail. Few mistakes. Dependable.

And she couldn't fall prey to the tugs he was making on her heart. Neediness had cost her part of her soul.

A part she'd never get back.

As she continued to stroke his hair, Audrey glanced around the bedroom. As pristine as the rest of his apartment, and as sparsely decorated, the room was what she would have expected of a man whose priority was not his home, but rather, in getting the sleep he needed to do his job.

A bed. A dresser. Another big-screen television—for those sleepless nights? No window treatments other than the standard white blinds that were on every window in the condo.

And in every other unit in the complex, as far she'd been able to tell.

Nothing that really spoke of the man's life. His past. No pictures of parents—or any other family. No obvious mementos from past girlfriends.

Not even a receipt on the dresser or a belt hanging from the doorknob.

He didn't put himself out there.

And that was just fine with her.

"I want to make love to you again." The words were uttered against her skin. Other than his mouth he hadn't moved.

And she was already filling up with the moist heat that

threatened to flood her lower belly. With a hand on his buttocks, she pulled him more fully inside her again.

"Then I think you should," she whispered, needing him so badly she ached for him.

But only physically.

Please, God, let it only be physical.

CHAPTER FIVE

RYAN GOT UP in time to make it to the meeting with Scott Markovich. The kid, fearing that his stepfather would hurt his mother if he was in detention and not there to protect her, admitted that the woman had been home the afternoon the bastard had come after Scott in a way a man should never come at a boy.

She'd been drinking since early morning and had been plastered enough that her husband thought he could get away with a little on the side with her son.

He'd miscalculated Scott's determination never to be touched that way again.

He'd also overestimated his wife's stupor. She'd come into the room soon enough to keep Scott from killing the son of a bitch.

And she'd promised him that from that moment forward she would never, ever let another drop of alcohol pass her lips.

Scott believed her.

Ryan didn't. As much as Scott wasn't going to like it at first, being separated from his mother was the best thing that could happen to the boy. There was a relative, an aunt on his father's side, who desperately wanted him.

None of that was Ryan's business, however. His

business here was almost done. A report to the prosecutor and he was out.

Another job done. A successful outcome this time.

Not something he ever took for granted.

Just as he didn't take for granted the woman who, on Saturday night, he was once again holding in his arms.

Not because he wanted to, but because he had to. His sudden need for Audrey was not something he was comfortable with. It didn't fit at all with his life plan. With his self-concept.

But one thing he'd learned in life—sometimes the things least understood were the most important.

"Thank you," she said now, her voice sleepy.

"For what?" They'd been talking for more than an hour, lying there naked in his bed, the covers up around their waists.

They'd been in bed almost three hours.

"For Scott."

He shrugged. "It's my job."

"Maybe."

There was no *maybe* about it.

"But there's something different about you. Something that makes you, I don't know, more accessible. I don't think Scott would have talked to anyone else. He's not very trusting of cops. As a rule, every time they've come around, his life has been painfully disrupted."

Because of his mother's drinking. And because when he'd reported his stepfather's earlier abuse, there hadn't been enough solid evidence to charge the man with anything. And now, when Scott had been defending himself from a horror that must have seemed worse than death to him, he'd been arrested and detained on charges of manslaughter.

They were all doing their jobs. Enforcing laws that were

in place to protect society, the people. So why was it so often that the victims were the ones who had the fewest rights?

With a brief flash of his birth mother, and a briefer one of his birth father—a man Ryan still struggled to accept for so many reasons on so many levels—Ryan said, "I think maybe my age helped us out this time. Most times it's the other way around."

He could say this here, to her. She'd understand. Audrey must have to fight many of the same battles he did, having so much responsibility, being capable of a maturity that was uncommon at such a young age.

Being forced into it by life's lessons.

Maybe someday, he'd even be able to tell her about the circumstances surrounding his conception.

Maybe someday. Not today. Other than a few brief conversations with the parents who'd raised him, Ryan hadn't talked about that particular case since they'd solved it the year before. Not even to the biological grandfather who was a law-enforcement icon in this state.

"How would your age have had anything to do with Scott's ability to trust you?" She turned onto her back, her head in the crook of his shoulder, pulling his hands around her to rest across the flatness of her belly.

"Maybe it doesn't. I just figured I'm probably closer to his age than any other detective he's had to deal with. I figured that might have helped him relate to me a little bit."

Her skull dug into his flesh as she turned to look up at him, grinning. "What, they give out some kind of memo at the office listing detectives' exact ages?" she asked.

"No." Suddenly Ryan wasn't feeling so good. Surely she knew...he just assumed she knew. Everyone seemed to.

Shit. What if she didn't know? His skin grew cold. Clammy. Worse than when he'd been facing that freaked-out druggie with the sawed-off shotgun the previous month.

"Then why would you say that?" she asked again. He could tell, from the frown marring her brow, the confusion in her gaze, that she was catching on to something.

And had no idea what.

Disentangling himself as gently, but as quickly, as possible, Ryan stood, skipping underwear as he pulled on his jeans and zipped them.

Surely this wouldn't be a big deal. She'd only be what, two, maybe three years older than he was, assuming she went straight from college to law school?

Suddenly the budding relationship he'd been fighting against became something he had to have. No matter what. And another one of life's little lessons became personal. Only by losing something—or facing its possible loss—did you realize its worth to you.

"You haven't heard them telling the jokes about the detective in diapers?" he asked, scrambling for words.

"*Nooo.*" She drew the word out, sitting up and pulling the covers to her chin. "Exactly how old are you, Ryan?"

"How old do you think I am?" Now that was a mature reply. Fresh out of junior high.

"I don't know. I thought early thirties. So…what…you're twenty-eight, twenty-nine? That's young for a full detective. And I guess it could make you seem more accessible to a kid Scott's age."

Ryan didn't lie. Or prevaricate. Or play games. He lived life by the rules. All of them.

If you didn't, people got hurt.

He was also a risk taker. Came with the cop territory.

He'd just never known such stark fear before when taking one.

"I'm twenty-two."

He faced her, an unarmed firing squad of one, and knew by the look on her face as soon as he said the words that he'd risked as much as he'd feared—and lost.

AT FIRST AUDREY THOUGHT he was joking. He had to be. She was not spending the weekend in bed with a twenty-two-year-old boy. Someone had paid him to say that. Except that Ryan wasn't the type to play mean games—not even for money. Especially not for money. If there was one thing she was sure of, it was that Ryan Mercedes could not be bought.

"Say something." He wasn't laughing.

He wasn't even smiling.

Nor did he look nonchalant, as though he was playing with her. In fact, he looked about as sick as she was beginning to feel. Sick, and scared.

And young.

Oh, God, what had she done?

"You're twenty-two." How could her voice sound like her when she'd just become someone she didn't know at all?

"Twenty-three in a little over seven months."

A young twenty-two. Not even twenty-two and a half. With numbers running quickly through her head, she stared at him, horrified.

Suddenly the sparseness of his apartment was no longer admirable. It screamed at her of youth and college and just starting out. The new patio furniture didn't make her feel warm and wanted, but rather, as though she'd come to a tea party with a child.

And lying there, naked in his bed, she felt like a sex offender. What would this young man's mother think of her?

She had to get up. Get dressed. Get out. Except that she didn't want him to see her naked. At twenty-two Ryan would be used to young, nubile, completely firm and unmarked coeds.

Audrey had cellulite.

And what in the hell did that matter?

She did not want to attract this kid. Didn't want him interested in her. At all. It was gross. She was gross.

Besides, he'd already seen it all.

When tears sprang to her eyes, she wanted to die.

"Hey, Audrey, it's not a big deal." With her eyes closed against the wetness still squeezing its way out of them to slide down her cheeks, Audrey almost gave in to that voice.

It had been the highlight of her life for weeks. It had brought her to life all weekend long, speaking to her of needs and a beauty that transcended all the trash their jobs brought to them. She'd responded to it like a flower to rain.

"Sweetie…"

Her heart calmed at the word. Knew a second of peace. Everything was going to be all right.

Then the bed dipped beneath his weight.

And she waited to feel the touch of his fingers on her face. Her neck. Needed to feel his heart beating beneath her cheek, his arms around her, keeping her safe…

No!

No! No! No! No! No!

"Stop!" The scream was shrill. Not a sound she'd ever

heard come out of her mouth before. "Don't come any closer." The tone was softer, but no less foreign.

"Come on, babe, it's not as if…"

Audrey's eyes flew open. Wide open. She held up a hand, silencing him. She knew now. Couldn't get sucked in by that deep, reassuring tone. The sense of confidence. How could she possibly find emotional safety and security with a twenty-two-year-old child?

Or almost child, she had to amend as she looked at the man sitting on the edge of the bed, concern shadowing his gaze. Concern and a caring so deep she almost couldn't breathe.

She knew the breadth of that chest intimately. Knew the strength in the bones and sinews. The gentleness and passion in his…

No! What in the hell was the matter with her?

His lack of chest hair wasn't genetic as she'd assumed. It was a symptom of youth. He hadn't grown any yet!

Good thing she knew where the bathroom was. She might need to make a dash for it if the nausea attacking her got any worse.

They'd showered together in there that morning. He'd soaped her back and breasts and…

"Don't *babe* me," she said with more strength in her voice. And some venom, too.

"You're angry." He sounded surprised, was sitting there wearing the most heart-wrenching frown. Compelling her to smooth it away with her fingers, followed by a kiss…

What was she? His damn mother? Needing to take care of his woes?

"Damn straight I'm angry." Audrey swung out of bed with a heave worthy of a football team, taking the covers with her. She would not expose her old body to his young gaze again.

Ever.

How embarrassing. Humiliating.

Wrong.

"Why? I don't get it." He followed her around the bed to where her clothes were scattered all over the floor. Helped her pick them up.

She snatched her bra from his fingers with a sharp "Give me that." He shook his head.

"What's a few years' difference in age, Audrey? We're still the same people who've been making love in that bed for most of the past twenty-four hours."

How dare he remind her of that? Especially now?

"A few years?" she screamed at him. Where *had* that voice come from? Taking a deep breath, she finished a little more calmly, "That's what you call it?"

"Last time I looked a few's three to four," he said, standing between her and the door—deliberately, she suspected. "I figure at the most we're looking at five or six, so if you want to split hairs and worry about semantics, then it's one or two more than a few."

His voice had lost some of its tenderness, though she detected no anger. Just distance. He was transforming from lover to detective again. From child to man. Audrey stared at him. She couldn't help it.

She had to leave. Had to get away and pretend this weekend never happened. To somehow rescue her heart from the debacle she'd created.

She started to laugh incredulously.

"Five or six years?" she asked, her voice, shaky with tears, still sharp. "That's what you think?"

He slid his hands into the pockets of his jeans. A child his age had no right to look so damned mature doing that.

So damned sexy.

"Yeah," he said with another frown. "You just took the bar exam. On average, a person graduates from college at twenty-one or -two, then does three years of law school. That puts him at twenty-five. But as smart as you are, and being a workaholic, I figured you probably didn't take five years to do your undergrad, so there's a good chance you were twenty or twenty-one when you finished your undergrad and twenty-three or -four out of law school, which made the difference in our ages not that great."

He'd given the matter a lot of thought. She didn't really understand why the notion calmed her, but she welcomed the respite. However brief it might turn out to be.

"I graduated from college at twenty," she told him, not sure her delivery carried the power she intended as she stood there trailing sheets and a blanket over her naked torso. "At which time I followed my mother's dictates and worked for her until I had saved enough money to attend law school without any help from her. She'd told me she would disown me if I made a decision so obviously not right for me."

Ryan's shoulders straightened. Tensed. His entire body seemed to be on alert. As though he were walking into a robbery in progress. "How long did it take you to save up for law school?"

"You can't work your first year in law school, did you know that?"

His eyes narrowed. "No."

"I had to save a couple of years' living expenses, as well as tuition and books…"

"But you were working for the boss, so you made a lot." There was nothing childlike about the alert man standing before her. Nothing young or immature about the commanding tone of voice, almost as though he could will the truth to be what he needed it to be.

"My mother insisted I start out at the bottom and earn my way up just like everyone else. Character building, she said."

She almost felt sorry for him. Except that she had to stay angry to survive this. And to figure out a way to exit with dignity.

Or, more importantly, with finality.

She just wasn't sure who she was mad at. Herself or him. She hadn't known. She'd assumed.

And so, apparently, had he.

Suddenly Audrey was exhausted. Needed to get this over and done with. Needed to get outside his world and find herself again.

To reassure herself that she was still there.

Intact.

That she hadn't made a mistake that would change the rest of her life.

"I'm thirty-five, Ryan." Her words were crisp and clear. All business. "Thirteen years older than you. Almost old enough to be your mother."

CHAPTER SIX

YOUR MOTHER. Audrey's words crashed around in Ryan's brain, deafening him to whatever else she was saying. He could see her lips moving, but couldn't make any sense out of the sound. *Your mother.*

She had no idea how close she was to the truth.

Ryan's biological mother was thirty-eight. Only three years older than the woman he'd spent the past twenty-four hours in bed with.

He stood rigid. It's what he did. Remained on his feet no matter the circumstances. Met it head on. Handled it.

Did what was right.

Followed the rules.

Black and white.

What in the hell did he do with a situation that had every color of the rainbow, in every hue, all clashing with one another, surrounded by a sea of brown and a buzzing that wouldn't quiet?

"Ryan, say something." She repeated his earlier words. They got through the cacophony.

"You're thirty-five," he said, only half-aware that he, too, repeated her earlier response.

"I can't believe you couldn't tell," she said. She looked so tiny standing there in bare feet, her slim shoulders naked above the tangle of covers she clutched around her. "I mean, I'm thirty-five. Not twenty."

"And?"

"My body doesn't look twenty."

The slight bit of insecurity that slipped through her tone, more than the statement itself, brought him back to the *them* he'd been a part of all weekend. Been a part of for months.

Audrey and Ryan. Two people who were meant for each other in some form.

"I have to go."

He couldn't let her walk out of his life. Regardless of his need to live it alone.

"Your body is beautiful," he told her. "Perfect. It drives me crazy with desire, turns me on almost to the point of selfishness, as this weekend's marathon session can attest to."

"I've never been with a less selfish man."

Her eyes had darkened, reeling him in, until her words landed. She was thirty-five years old. There had been others.

Undoubtedly with a lot more experience.

Growing warm despite the chills climbing the back of his neck, an unfamiliar lack of confidence creeping up his spine, Ryan continued to stand there. He didn't have any other method of operation.

"I've never been with another woman."

He could have kicked himself. Why in the hell had he said that? What possible bearing could it have on the current situation?

Except perhaps to seal his fate, showing himself for the kid she was making him feel like.

Damn it. He saved lives for a living. Looked after two sets of parents. Risked his life every single day.

Society relied on him to keep them secure. His superiors respected him. Trusted him. Knew he'd get the job done.

"You're kidding, right?"

Here was his chance. One word and he could get some of his pride back. *Right.* That's all he had to say.

Except that it wouldn't be right. Ryan didn't lie. He didn't shy away from tough situations. He didn't settle or compromise. He upheld black and white so that the citizens of Columbus could sleep at night.

"No."

"You're gorgeous, Ryan! And the most virile, passionate man I've ever met. There's no way you made it through twenty-two years of living without some girl offering to take care of you."

"She offered."

"And you said no."

"Yes."

"Why?" Head tilted, she watched him. "You weren't attracted enough to her?" The honest curiosity in her eyes, mixed with a bit of incredulity in her tone, compelled his answer.

"I wasn't in love with her."

"And?"

"Lovemaking, by its very definition, requires love."

He knew exactly what he was telling her. And said the words, anyway. Black and white. That's how he lived. Even if the facts staring him in the face were hard to take.

"No guy waits for love his first time. Or any time for that matter."

"I'm the exception that proves the rule, I guess."

"You didn't want her."

"Oh, I did." He nodded, remembering how physically painful it had been to turn Mary Ellen away. She'd followed him into the kitchen of his apartment one night shortly after he'd moved in. He'd intended to throw some popcorn in the microwave for the movie they were about to watch.

She'd unbuttoned her top, and the snap on her jeans....

"I don't get it."

He wasn't going to explain it to her. Not right now, at any rate. "Let's just say that I have a clear understanding of what damage can be done when one has sex for the wrong reasons. Taking a chance on hurting someone who said she was in love with me when I knew I wasn't in love with her, just for a few minutes of physical gratification, was not worth the lack of self-respect I'd have later."

"Unbelievable."

"Mine is the only face I see when I look in the mirror in the morning. It's up to me to keep it clean."

"People have sex all the time without love. *Like* is nice, but even that's not necessary in today's world."

Was she telling him something? If so, he wasn't sure he wanted to know. Not if it meant that the experience they'd shared meant nothing more to her than good sex.

"Just because I've got a penis doesn't mean that I can be irresponsible with it."

As she'd been with her vagina? As much as she might want him to believe that—and he wasn't sure she did—she could be speaking generally. He couldn't see Audrey giving herself lightly.

She'd been emotionally engaged with him. He wasn't going to accept any other version of what they'd shared.

"I've never met anyone like you." Her tone had softened distinctly.

Ryan took one step closer. "Nor I you."

Tilting her head to meet his gaze, Audrey started to speak and stopped. Age didn't erase the lost waif confusion from her eyes. Or the trembling from her lips.

She hadn't called him on his backhanded declaration of love.

"I was afraid you'd be able to tell it was my first time."

"Uh-uh." She shook her head without breaking eye contact. "You were incredible. Why would you think that?"

"I came so soon."

"The first time, but anyone would have after all the touching we did beforehand."

"You didn't just have sex with me because it felt good," he said.

"No."

"Your heart was involved."

She turned her head away, burying her face in her shoulder. And he breathed the first easy breath since the entire conversation began.

It was still there—whatever it was they were to each other. Right now he was too relieved to know that to care about the danger of losing his autonomy.

"Audrey." With a gentle finger he lifted her chin. "It's okay."

"No," she said with trembling lips, a trembling voice, "it's not okay, Ryan. I'm thirteen years older than you. A whole different generation. Nothing's ever going to change that."

"So we have some unexpected challenges we'll have to face," he said slowly, leaning toward her. Another inch and their bodies would be touching again.

Every nerve he possessed needed the contact.

"Life is full of challenges," he continued. He had to have her in his life. He had to be alone. White and black inside him at the same time.

What in the hell was he doing?

What could he do?

She licked her lips.

And he said, "We're still the same people we were last month. Last week. And last night."

What was he saying?

He couldn't possibly bring a thirty-five-year-old woman home to meet his parents.

Either set of them.

Eyes wide, she stared at him as though he were a lifeline. Her only hope out of a nightmare that wouldn't end.

That look resonated within him, knocking him off any sense of direction he might have thought he had. She was *his* hope.

And he had to protect her. Period.

"Right," she said, an unfamiliar note of bitterness in her voice. "I want children, Ryan. Tell me how we'd meet that challenge."

Children. With her. Having kids of his own wasn't something he'd given much thought to. Except to know that it was way down the road.

But having children with Audrey? It seemed natural. A given. Like he should have known all along.

Like he'd left himself and was living the life of another man.

"What?" he said, needing to take her shoulders, to hold her there right where he knew she needed to be—and sensing that if he did, he could lose her. "You think my sperm's different from some thirty-five- or forty-year-old guy's? I'm going to produce some inferior kid?" he asked, being deliberately obtuse.

He couldn't argue her point. The obstacles in front of them seemed insurmountable. He needed some time to find the way over them. Around them. Through them.

Or a way out. For both of them.

"I have to go." She glanced away.

Cupping her shoulders, Ryan said, "Audrey."

"I cannot stand here and discuss having babies with you, Ryan. You *are* a baby."

That stung. "Oh, so the guy who made you scream with ecstasy less than two hours ago, who was he?"

"Ryan."

"Or how about the one who talked Scott Markovich into saving his own ass by turning in his mother?"

"That's different."

"Oh, I get it. It's okay that I risk my life every day for the people in this city, but I'm just too young to live that life. If it ends when I go to work tomorrow night, then so be it. I wasn't old enough to live it, anyway."

"Ryan!"

"I'm grown-up enough to carry a weapon, several of them, to help protect you and everyone else in this town from the dregs of humanity. I'm man enough to take on consci-enceless, drugged-out, maniacal murderers and rapists and child molesters, just not man enough to love?"

"Stop it." There was a hint of begging in her tone.

"Why? Because I'm getting too close to the truth for you to handle?" He couldn't seem to shut up. Which was so unlike him. He could hear his anger and frustration, knew he had to stifle himself before he said something he'd regret and have to atone for. "What's the real truth here, Audrey? Is it that you're older than me? Or that you've had a great weekend, maybe the best you've ever had, and you're scared? Because tomorrow you're going to have to go home, go back to the real world and face the fact that I might have been playing with you? That *you* might actually get hurt rather than being the woman who's always helping heal other people's hurts?"

Her chin rose. "I don't have to listen to that." She didn't step away.

"I think you do," he said, not budging, either. "I get that this isn't going to be a normal relationship. We're going to raise some eyebrows. And probably have an occasional generational blip—like I'm guessing you don't know who One Republic is. But in the large scheme of things, looking at life and death and happiness and love, none of that matters."

"Of course it matters!" Audrey's shoulders drooped as though the energy it took to get out that sentence was all she had left. With a couple of sloppy swooshes, she moved back to the edge of the bed. Sat.

Ryan wanted to join her. Wasn't sure he should. And this was what she'd brought him to? A man who was so unsure of himself all of a sudden that he couldn't decide whether or not to sit on his own bed?

He sat, close enough that his arm was touching hers. If he was going to do something, he was damn well going to do it all the way. If he made a mistake, he'd make it big.

"We can sit here and pretend all we want to, Ryan, but there is no way we can ignore the ramifications of a thirty-five-year-old woman taking up with a twenty-two-year-old man. Think of what people will say! And I can guarantee you, they'll be a whole lot more negative about me than about you."

"So? We're going to let strangers' opinions determine our lives?"

"They'd call you my boy-toy."

"And?"

"It's disgusting."

"So? It hurts us how?"

"I don't want people thinking things like that about either one of us."

"I'm not that bad-looking, Audrey," he couldn't keep from reminding her. "Some folks might actually envy you. Hell, they're probably going to think you're an amazing woman to catch the attention of a young stud like me."

A smile started at the corner of her mouth, then she looked at him. Studied him. And her face fell.

"Yeah, and follow that one through," she said softly. "How attracted to me are you still going to be when I'm forty-five and menopausal and starting to sag and you're thirty-two and virile and some twenty-five-year-old beauty is falling all over you?"

"If I'm with you, I'm not going to be close enough to any other female for her to have the opportunity to fall all over me."

"You're human, Ryan."

"I'm also *me*. I don't cross those lines."

"You don't know that!" With her fists still clenched in the covers, she pounded her thigh. "This is my point, Ryan. You're only twenty-two. You haven't lived long enough yet, haven't had enough experience yet to know how you'd react in a situation like that."

"Oh, so there's some magical chart that tells when a man's lived long enough to know himself? To know what kind of choices he makes in life? Do I need to live longer to know that I'm not going to rape a woman? Or rob a bank? Or murder my next-door neighbor?"

"Why do you keep doing this?" Her eyes were moist as she looked at him again. Those naked shoulders were making it hard for him to keep his hands to himself. He needed to pull her into his arms. Comfort her until she was smiling and energetic again.

Hold her until she was happy.

"I'm not letting you walk out of my life," he told her simply. "I don't see a reason worthy of how wrong that would be."

"Ryan. Go call your parents. Tell them that you're seeing a woman who's thirty-five years old. Go on. Do it."

Thinking of his adoptive parents, Harriet and Glen, their simple lives, he blanched. They knew him. Protected him where they could. Accepted his aloneness. What in the hell was he thinking?

Then he looked at Audrey and his heart took over once again. Putting him on a course he didn't choose, didn't understand, but couldn't deny.

"In the first place, I can't call them," he said. "It's midnight and they'll be asleep." At least the parents who raised him would be. Mark and Sara, his biologicals, tended to be late-night people. Ryan liked to think it was because of the baby, but knew it was more than that. Mark still had problems sleeping at night.

Came from spending too many years in a prison cell.

"In the second place, no matter how hard you try, you are not going to make me into a little boy. I'm of age, Audrey. I do not have to call my parents for permission for anything. Nor am I in the habit of doing so."

Standing, Audrey reached for her clothes, stepping into the pants she'd changed into earlier that day when they'd stopped by her home on the way to see Markovich. "Look, Ryan, I know you mean well, but—"

"Don't humor me," he interrupted, standing, as well. "I'm still Detective Mercedes. You know, the one whose capabilities you respect?"

His tone stopped her, midway through fastening her bra. "I know you are," she said, looking him straight in the eye. "And I know I'm confused," she continued. "I just need to go home, try to sort all this out. I need to get some sleep."

"You think you're going to sleep?"

"Honestly?"

"Of course."

"No. But I'm going to lie in my bed, like I do every other night of my life, and try."

"I'm not giving up on us," Ryan said, holding her blouse for her as she slipped her arms inside. This would not be the last time he saw this woman's skin, the last time his knuckles brushed her stomach.

"There is no *us*."

That stung. "You're the one who mentioned babies."

"I was speaking hypothetically." Bending, she slipped into the high-heeled sandals she'd left at the end of the bed. "Pointing out the impossibilities."

"You never actually got around to doing that," he reminded her, fully aware that he was being somewhat irascible at the moment. Acting like the brat she thought him? "Tell me why I'm not capable of fathering your child."

"There's a whole lot more to fathering a child than impregnating its mother." Audrey's voice sounded weary as she headed for the stairs. "Do you have any idea how awkward it would be for a child to have to live with peoples' exclamations every single time he introduced them to his parents?"

"Oh, we'd be wearing signs, then? With our ages scrolled across our chests? Just like Hawthorne's scarlet *A?*"

"No, but—"

"But what, Audrey?" His stomach knotted as he followed her down the stairs. What if this was it? What if he couldn't get her to come back? "When you were a kid, did people ask you how old your mother was?"

"No!"

"Did either of us notice a difference in our ages by looking at us?"

"No."

"And we even saw each other naked." He just had to bring that up. Had to remind her who they were, what they'd done together. Created together.

"But with time—"

"I'll dye my hair gray if it'll make you feel better. Or you can keep yours blond. We'll exercise and eat right. I'll spend more time in the sun so I wrinkle prematurely."

They were downstairs and she wasn't stopping. She grabbed her purse without missing a step and turned to the entryway. He had to do something.

Had to stop this from happening.

"Think about this," he said, scrambling for anything that might help. "The average life expectancy of men in the United States is seventy-something. That skews younger if you have a job like mine. For women life expectancy is eighty-something. That's where the buck stops and puts us just about even."

At his front door, her hand on the knob, Audrey turned to him. "Ah, Ryan, why do you have to be so determined?"

Several smart remarks sprang to mind. Mostly along the lines of *That's what I'd like to know.* But the words came from someplace inside him. "Because this matters. You matter."

He knew he'd scored—at least a chance—when she nodded. "I'll call you tomorrow."

"Call me tonight." When it looked as though she was going to argue, he continued, "I won't pick up, I promise. Just leave me a message letting me know you're home safely."

At her acquiescence, Ryan walked her out, saw her safely into the front seat of her blue Acura.

He bent to kiss her, fully expected her to turn her head, and was thrilled when she didn't. The effect of her lips on his rent through his entire system.

Body. Mind. And heart.

He had it bad.

"And by the way," she offered, starting her engine as he was pushing her door closed.

He stopped midway.

"One Republic hit number four on the pop rock charts last October with a song called 'Apologize.' They were big news because their debut album wasn't out until November. Even us old folks, hard of hearing as we are, listen to the radio occasionally."

With that, she pulled her door closed, put the car in Drive and sped away.

Ryan missed her already.

CHAPTER SEVEN

SHE CALLED as she'd promised she would. And as he'd promised, Ryan didn't pick up. Audrey had known he wouldn't. Ryan Mercedes always did what he said he was going to do. It was one of the things she loved about him.

Loved, as in *was fond of*. Like a friend. Or a highly respected work associate.

That she'd slept with. Once. After some wine. A twenty-four-hour sleep.

A twenty-four-hour aberration that would not—could not—be given any validity whatsoever. That meant no thinking about it. Analyzing it.

Missing it.

He phoned on Sunday. She let the answering machine pick up. She'd said she'd call him, but that was before agreeing to call last night. Which she'd done. That bit of communication had stood in the stead of the original promise. Or so she worked it out.

He apparently thought differently, judging by his message.

"Audrey. It's ten o'clock. I'm leaving for work in a few minutes. You said you'd call. I've been waiting all day. I hope you're all right. Call me."

She stood staring at the machine, listening. And she'd

have been just fine if he'd ended it there as she'd thought he was going to do.

Turning away, determination still intact, his final word reached out and hooked her.

"Please."

It was the worry in his voice that did it.

There was something compelling, addictive even, in having someone worry about you. Especially when you were as unused to the practice as she was.

She'd often thought, if only her mother had worried about her a little more, Audrey would have been so much happier doing the older woman's bidding. She'd have tried to please her mom out of love, instead of out of fear. Or emotional manipulation.

She waited until ten-forty-five—the time he'd be in the meeting that was the precursor to every work shift—then dialed his cell phone.

"Hi, it's Audrey." Her voice sounded loud in her too quiet home. "I'm fine. Have a great week. Bye."

Ryan was a smart man. Boy. That oughtta do it.

After a day filled with client meetings—which meant stopping by homes to check up on kids—and studying and writing reports in her small downtown office, Audrey went to bed shortly after the call to Ryan. She was exhausted and tomorrow was Monday. The beginning of a new week.

A new life.

She didn't sleep well that night.

"YOU LOOK TIRED. You really should do more with yourself. Exercise. Eat better. Wear that night cream I bought you."

"I walked on the treadmill for an hour last night," Audrey

told the older woman sitting across from her in the upscale seafood restaurant Thursday night. She'd put in an hour every day this week. Usually somewhere between one and four in the morning.

"What about eating? How many times have you had potatoes or pasta this week?"

I'm thirty-five years old. You don't own me anymore. "None."

"Well, that's something. I've never met anyone who loves starches as much as you do. It's not becoming in a woman."

Audrey promptly dropped the piece of French bread she'd been nibbling. You'd think, listening to her mother, that she was a porker, obese.

"I know that carbs are good for you," her mother continued, picking a cucumber from her salad with two perfectly manicured fingers. "Recent studies show that it's probably those complex carbs you eat that are keeping you slim—"

"And heart-healthy and non-diabetic," Audrey interjected, just to let her mother know that she'd listened the last umpteen times she'd heard this lecture. Or maybe just to add the occasional sound of her own voice.

"Yes, well, you still look tired. You work too much."

As if she hadn't put in eighteen-hour days when she worked in retailing for her mother, who ran a distribution business for high-end women's accessories, as well as a small, upscale boutique.

"I've got a couple of difficult cases," she said. One in particular she'd like her mother's opinion on.

If she could find a way to ask for it without actually asking. She didn't want a lecture. Just thoughts.

"I told you you weren't made out for that difficult life.

You should never have gone to law school. If you'd stayed with us, you'd have your own department by now."

Which would be great if she was enthused by jewelry and clothes.

Audrey smiled, Eyed the bread she couldn't touch.

"I stopped by last weekend. You weren't home."

"I was with clients."

Amanda set down her fork with careful precision and lifted her gaze, pointing it straight at Audrey.

"It was late. Past ten. On Friday night."

Dammit, Audrey was thirty-five, not fourteen. She lifted her chin. "I had a date."

"A date." Amanda, completely straight-faced, continued to stare. "With who?"

"A detective I met working a case a few months back." Audrey picked her words deliberately, figuring her mother would find fault with her date's career choice and that would be the end of that.

Detective jobs were too dangerous. What woman in her right mind would want to saddle herself with someone who could easily die on the job? Or bring danger home?

She'd heard her mother's voice in her head, saying just those things, during the weeks she'd been seeing Ryan.

Before she'd found out he was little more than a child.

"And?"

"And what?"

"So? How'd it go?"

The bread was tempting. So tempting. "Good. Fine."

"You going to see him again?"

"I don't think so."

Her mother picked up her fork, stabbed a wedge of

lettuce. "Typical man," she retorted. "Gets what he wants, then leaves you hanging out to dry."

Audrey almost grabbed the bread. "Why would you assume he got what he wanted?"

Amanda's brown eyes opened wide. "Didn't he?"

Audrey had walked right into that one.

"I drove by again around six in the morning." Amanda relented. "You weren't home then, either."

Exasperated on so many levels, Audrey had to resist the urge to get up and walk out.

"What were you doing out at six in the morning?" she blurted. She didn't know who the uncharacteristic response shocked more, her or her mother. "Why were you checking up on me?" Her mind stumbled over thoughts that were clamoring for release. Really, this was too much. Even for Amanda Lincoln. The audacity of the woman! "And why didn't you say anything when I spoke to you on Sunday?"

"I was waiting for you to tell me about him," Amanda said, calmly chewing her salad.

"It didn't have to be a guy," Audrey wished she had something a little stronger than the diet soda she always ordered when she was driving. "I could have been at the hospital."

"My number's in your wallet in case of emergency," Amanda reminded her.

"Anyway—" Audrey couldn't seem to shut up "—you didn't tell me why you were out."

"Don't get mouthy with me, girl."

"Answer my question, Mom."

"I couldn't sleep."

"So you drove half an hour to my place?"

"It's not a crime."

For once Amanda seemed more interested in the table-cloth than her prey. Audrey frowned.

"How often do you do that?"

With a shrug, her mother motioned a passing waiter for some more water.

"Mom?"

"I don't know. Sometimes."

"Why?"

"Why not? Driving helps. I have to go somewhere."

"You check up on me on a regular basis."

"So what if I do?" Amanda's tone, her gaze, sharpened. "I'm your mother."

"Because you don't trust me, even at thirty-five, to live my own life." Audrey reached for her bag. This was ludicrous.

"Because I care about you." Shocked at the sudden drop in her mother's voice, Audrey stilled. Watched the older woman. "I worry about you living all alone."

No other words could have worked in that moment. Audrey's heart softened. "I'm fine, Mom. I've got an alarm system. You know that."

"Yes, well." Amanda returned her attention to her salad. "How well did you do, staying with a man who dumped you afterward?"

Any other day, Audrey would have let that go. "He didn't dump me."

Amanda stared. "But you said you weren't going to see him again."

"That's right."

"You didn't like him? What was wrong with him? My God, Audrey, you're thirty-five years old. How do you think it makes me feel to have to keep telling people that my daughter isn't married yet? They're going to start thinking something's wrong with you. Besides, your clock is ticking. And so is mine."

A new line. "What does your clock have to do with anything?"

"What if I want grandkids?"

That got her attention. "Do you?"

"Not particularly. Raising you alone was hard enough."

"Then why does age matter?"

"Because I'm not getting younger." Amanda's tone changed once again, as did her focus. It was anywhere but on Audrey as she added, "I'm not going to be around forever to take care of you, you know."

With absolutely no idea what to do with that, or the sudden worry the words instilled, Audrey said, albeit gently, "So I'm supposed to hook up with someone I don't want to be with?"

Oh, God, Ryan. Forgive me. But I don't want to be with a boy almost young enough to be my son. The ramifications terrify me. She glanced again at her mother. "You chose to live your life alone."

"I had you."

As if that made all the difference? Had Amanda ever stopped to think about how focusing her entire attention on Audrey wasn't healthy? For either of them?

Their dinner arrived and Audrey tried to find enough appetite to approach the scallops she'd ordered. Avoiding the mashed potatoes that came with them wasn't even going to be an issue tonight. The sight of them almost choked her.

"So what was wrong with this guy?"

Fifteen minutes had passed.

"He's…immature."

"And?"

"That's it."

Fork in midair, Amanda studied her. "You're kidding, right? Audrey, honey, all men are immature."

No, actually, they weren't. Some were simply young. She cut a scallop in half. Got it to her lips. Inside her mouth. Started to chew.

"Anyway, what does he do that's so immature?"

Swallowing took effort. Concentration. She managed. "He…calls," she said, trying to keep her mind off the subject at hand. A feat she'd been attempting, without impressive success, all week. "Every night." Like a kid who didn't know when to quit.

"Well, honey! That means he really likes you! For a grown man to call a woman that much in this day and age…I think that's sweet." The sudden lift in Amanda's voice, the surprise, was almost insulting. "What do you talk about?"

"Nothing. I don't pick up."

"Audrey! That's rude."

She preferred to think of it as survival.

"What if he stops calling?"

The question, one she'd refused to allow voice to—even mental voice—all week, struck her heart. "I'm counting on it," she finally managed with a semblance of calm.

"Does he leave messages?"

If you wanted to call a ten-minute-long, one-sided conversation a message. "Yeah."

"Saying what? Does he want to see you again? Has he asked you out for this weekend?"

More like, he'd asked her in. He'd said they could spend the entire weekend at his place, or hers, if that would make her feel better about people not seeing her with a younger man. As if hiding away for a weekend would do anything but make the entire situation more impossible, more painful, later. An oversight that was a product of his youth.

"He asked me to call him."

"Did you?"

"No."

"But you're going to, right?"

"No."

"Audrey. Yes, you are. You must have liked him or you wouldn't have spent the night with him. Don't forget. This is me you're talking to. I know you."

Amanda had her there. And because Audrey couldn't argue with the woman, she shut up and ate her scallops. Remembering the past—the irrevocable choices.

The reasons she could never, ever love a man as black and white as Ryan Mercedes. Or as young. What would happen when time started to show on her face and she was no longer as attractive as she was, but he was? Would she resort to begging him for his love and affection? As she'd done with her mother?

She couldn't risk it.

Never again would she dare put herself in a position where she'd compromise herself because she needed to be loved.

MARCUS RYAN had been asleep for more than an hour. The little guy was only a couple of months old and still up every couple of hours for feedings. Ryan peered over the edge of the bassinet for the fourth time Thursday evening. Just checking. Just to be sure.

Then he lay back on the end of the couch closest to the

infant's portable bed—moved from the master bedroom, to home office, to living room through the course of the day— and listened to his baby brother breathe.

Only for a while. A moment out of time because Sara had needed him. And because he had a guaranteed escape—a job that required he live opposite to the rest of the world.

Odd that he'd find comfort in those innocent gushes of air. And a sense of belonging he'd never known before.

And tonight, there was more. A longing he didn't fully understand. For Audrey. For family. And for a peace too elusive for him to grasp.

Or fully believe in.

Ten o'clock, escape—from confusion, from longing, from all of them—couldn't come fast enough.

HER PHONE didn't ring at ten-fifteen Thursday night. Or at ten-thirty. He didn't call her on the way to work as he'd done all week. Or even right before he went into his preshift briefing. Not that she'd have answered.

At five after eleven, when she knew he'd be firmly ensconced in the job and not be calling her, Audrey ran a hot bubble bath. Poured herself a glass of wine. Grabbed some chocolates out of the refrigerator, an aged stash that was to be consumed only in an emergency, lit a couple of candles and settled in to enjoy herself.

To celebrate.

She'd succeeded.

She was free.

AT ELEVEN-FORTY-FIVE Thursday night, she was still in the tub. The water was only lukewarm, but she could lean forward at any moment, twist the knob and make it hot again. Her glass was empty. The candy melting. And the candles were flickering, their wicks buried in puddles of liquid wax ready to suffocate them at any second.

She didn't feel good yet. But she would.

Ryan had finally given up. Decided to leave her alone. Life would settle down now. Get easier. Just the way she wanted it.

And she wanted it desperately.

AT HALF-PAST MIDNIGHT Friday morning, lying sleepless in her bed, Audrey ignored the damp puddles on her pillow, ignored the tightness in her chest, the weight in her stomach. She ignored the taunting from the critic in her brain.

Of course more than a lifetime of loneliness and work awaited her. She was going to be fine. Better than fine. In a minute or two, a day or two. Okay, maybe a week or two, she'd be as good as new. Happy, confident.

Or at least content.

She'd be fully in control of her life and the decisions she had to live with forever. No longer in danger of giving up self for love.

And maybe she'd find some nice, mature older man to spend some time with. A man who had no interest in anything more committed than an occasional companion, a good friendship, a man who'd already had wife and family, who, perhaps, had grown children.

She was human and had been alone too long, had been starved for companionship. That was why Ryan had affected her so deeply. Her reactions to him, her supposed caring for him, had been nothing more than proximity.

Please, God, make it so, she begged silently.

Someone else, someone younger and more appropriate for him, would see Ryan's unique gifts, would appreciate his loyalty and would value the way he always did what he said he'd do. Someone else would thrill over the pleasure his body gave. Someone else would make certain that he was loved and cherished every day of his life. He would be fine.

"Stop it!"

She sat up, clutching her pillow to her chest.

"Stop this right now. You're torturing yourself."

Her voice, cracked and ragged—and loud in the quiet of her house—didn't bring her back to her senses. It hurt her more. Until she wondered if she *was* going to survive. If she did know what she was doing.

About anything.

If she knew anything.

What in the hell was she doing, crying over a man/child she'd only known a few months—and slept with once? For a weekend.

What in the hell was the matter with her?

Audrey might have come up with an answer. She hadn't been planning to lie down again anytime soon. Couldn't stand the agony she was putting herself through.

She might have come up with an answer…but the phone rang.

CHAPTER EIGHT

MAYBE IT HAD BEEN A juvenile thing to do, waiting until he'd been on shift for a couple of hours before calling her. Making her wonder if he *would* call. Hoping to force her to pick up by calling in the middle of the night.

Listening to her phone ring, unanswered, his heart pounding harder the closer he got to five rings, to speaking to the answering machine again, Ryan forced his mind to the information at hand.

A confirmation he'd just, in the past five seconds, received.

It didn't matter that she wasn't answering her phone in the middle of the night. Didn't matter that she might not be there. That she might be sharing another man's bed.

Depressing his finger on the end key, he terminated the call before her machine picked up.

It was for the best. He could get his life back under control. Be free to be alone without all the emotional rigamarole making him nuts. Making him into something he was not.

Maybe she was in the bathroom. Couldn't get to the phone. Maybe he should give her one more chance.

Hitting redial, he waited for the line to connect.

She might have shared the other guy's bed before Ryan, too. She was thirty-five years old. There had been others. Probably before Ryan had even had his first wet dream.

Audrey Lincoln's life was her own. She'd made that fact quite plain over the past five days.

And really, she'd never given him indication to believe otherwise. She'd never confessed her love for him. Or even her loyalty.

One ring and counting.

She'd had sex with him.

Didn't mean that it in any way resembled, for her, the life-changing experience it had been for him.

Hell, she was thirty-five, experienced.

Three rings.

He was acting like the kid he was, thinking that those hours in his bed had been something special. Momentous.

Four rings.

He'd lost his virginity. Nothing more.

Five rings.

It was about time. Who'd ever heard of a virgin cop?

"You've reached…" Waiting for her message to finish, Ryan closed his eyes. He could join in the locker-room talk at the station now. Not.

"Audrey, this is Ryan Mercedes. Listen, I've got some information for you regarding your father. If you're interested, give me a call. If not, forgive the intrusion."

Hanging up, Ryan still didn't regret having known the woman.

How dare he?

How dare he?

Fuming, pacing, the hardwood floors cold on her bare feet even in July, Audrey tried to calm herself.

Just as she'd thought, Ryan Mercedes was a kid. Didn't

know the proper boundaries between adults. What had possessed him to trespass on her private territory, her life, so intimately? He'd looked up her father?

If she'd wanted to find the man, she could have done so herself. He'd paid child support.

Someone could have traced him through that. No matter that the money came in the form of cashier's checks, with different signatures, from various states, throughout the years of her growing up.

Damn him!

If she'd wanted to deal with her father, she'd have said so. What on earth gave him the idea she'd want that?

What gave him the idea he'd had any right to jump so completely into her life?

Hadn't his mother taught him anything about respecting people's privacy?

She paced, rubbing her shoulders against the cold blowing from air conditioners set in windows in the different rooms of her little home on the hill. Her sleeveless nightgown had been fine in her bed.

Who cared about her father?

The man had deserted her long ago.

Too long ago.

Leaving her to deal with her mother's unique charms all on her own. A defenseless kid against a manipulative woman who'd ruled her world with threats, rather than love.

A woman who'd blackmailed and coerced and forced, rather than guided. Audrey hadn't had a chance.

And would pay the consequences, live with the heartbreak and shame, for the rest of her life.

Damn the man who'd fathered her. He should have pulled out a couple of minutes sooner.

And damn Ryan, too.

Damn them all.

She didn't need a man. *Any* man. And she'd show them just that. She'd ignore Ryan's call. He could keep his information.

And everything else he thought he had to offer.

RYAN SWEATED IT OUT the rest of Thursday night. He worked, focusing on the bigger picture of his life, the contribution he had to make to the world that had taken him on, the world that gave him air to breathe, food to eat, songs to hear and beauty to enjoy.

What he didn't do was get in his department-issued sedan and take a run through a certain Westerville neighborhood, past a particular guardian ad litem's home. So she worked in sometimes dangerous situations, pissing off sometimes dangerous people. So she lived alone. She had an alarm.

And there were officers out there whose job it was to see that the neighborhoods were safe.

Patrol, checking up, wasn't part of his job anymore.

He didn't get to prevent crimes anymore. Only to explain. And prevent repeat offenses.

So be it.

All night long, it was.

And on the way home Friday morning, he took no detour. Whether or not she'd been out all night—even if he could tell with a drive-by—was none of his business.

Home in record time, he fed his cat, patted her on the head—something he constantly forgot she hated—climbed the stairs and fell into his unmade bed fully clothed.

Ryan Mercedes was back.

THE CHILD LOOKED ILL. Lab reports had all come back that she was healthy. There was no medical explanation for her fatigue. Psychological assessments found her to be a normal twelve-year-old. She had all the right answers. But she wasn't doing well in school. Not surprising, due to the custody battle being fought over her.

Sitting across from Carrie Woods in a booth at the ice-cream shop around the corner from the girl's father's house Friday morning, Audrey wished she could spirit the child away.

"I love my mom, Ms. Lincoln," she said, her eyebrows drawn together in an expression far too mature for her age. Her brown eyes were shadowed with unshed tears. "I love her so much."

"Of course you do, honey."

"And I love my daddy, too."

"You're supposed to."

"It hurts my mom."

Listening with more than just ears to her new client, Audrey heard something that resonated deeply. Was she looking at another young girl who had to earn her mother's love?

"How so?"

"My dad hurt her so badly and she hates him, and when I love him she thinks I'm turning traitor on her."

When, in fact, my dear sweet child, your mother is turning traitor on you. It was against the law for a woman to leave her kids locked safely at home while she went out to try to earn money for food—they called it child endangerment—but it wasn't against the law for a selfish woman to have a child and then take away its right to life by depriving it of love.

"So when she says you don't want these week-long summer visitations with your father, she's not being entirely accurate?"

"I don't want them."

Audrey heard herself telling a doctor she wanted a procedure. And felt sick.

She looked Carrie straight in the eye. "Why don't you want them?"

Silence.

"Is he mean to you?"

Eyes opening wider, Carrie shook her head, her blond hair falling in angelic curls around her slim shoulders. The girl was wearing a brown tank top that perfectly matched her eyes. And a pair of short, beige shorts. Simple. But expensive-looking. Her hair was clean. Combed.

"My dad loves me."

That was important. The fact that the child knew that even more so.

She'd known about the procedure, too. Known that the choice was wrong for her.

"What about his girlfriend?"

"She's nice, too. I like her."

"Do they ignore you, then? Leave you alone too much?"

For the first time since she'd been introduced to the child that morning, Audrey heard her chuckle. "Sometimes I wish they would!" she said. "At home I spend a lot of time in my room. I like to read and write in my journal. But here, we're always doing stuff. I haven't finished a single book all week."

So they made her do things she didn't want to do? Was that what she'd been called in to discover? Audrey didn't think so.

"What kinds of things?" she asked, anyway. She couldn't take any chances, couldn't risk superimposing her own issues on her charges.

Empathizing was good. Understanding, vital. Mistaking the facts, unforgivable.

"Oh, you know, stuff you do when you're on vacation. We went to King's Island. And we go to the pool. My dad's teaching me how to dive off the high board. And Kelly—that's his girlfriend—and I are working on a cross-stitch thing. She's teaching me how."

"Do you like it?"

Carrie's nod was more hesitant.

"Not that much?"

"Well…" The child looked down at the ice cream melting in her bowl, then up again, the shadows back in her eyes. "Actually, I do like it. Really a lot. It's just that…"

Carrie liked going to her dad's. Audrey hadn't wanted the procedure. But they both told a different story.

For the same reason.

"What?" she asked, needing Carrie to admit what Audrey already knew.

"I can't bring it home with me or anything."

"Kelly won't let you take it?"

"Yeah, she wants me to. She wants to see how good I do between now and when I come back in two weeks."

"So what's the problem?" Audrey felt the old familiar knot in her stomach, figuring Carrie would recognize it completely, figuring that a similar knot had become the young girl's constant companion.

Audrey had carried hers for most of her life.

"It would make my mom cry."

Because another woman was "mothering" her daughter. An understandable challenge to overcome. An understandable pain.

And yet, as a mother, it was Mrs. Woods's job to see that that pain didn't spill over onto her daughter's life.

"And then what?"

"She wouldn't love me."

"Of course she would," Audrey said, more because the little girl needed to hear it than because she believed it. "Let me talk to her," Audrey said. "I'm sure, once I explain how much you love her and that you can't help loving your dad, too, once she knows that you're hurting so much over this, she won't have any problem with you bringing your cross-stitching home."

Or with you coming back to see your father, either, Audrey added silently.

"You don't know my mom," Carrie said, her shoulders slumped almost to the table.

"I know that she wants what's best for you," Audrey said, understanding far too well the weight this little girl was carrying. And she knew that either the mother was going to change her method of operation or Audrey would be recommending a change in custody for her daughter.

Carrie wasn't going to someday find herself facing a doctor she didn't want to see. Or making any other life-changing choices that weren't right for her because she felt she had to, to be loved.

FRIDAY AFTERNOON, following lunch with a couple of board members from the Ohio Guardian Ad Litem Association to discuss a training event she was going to be administering,

Audrey took a detour on the way back to her office. Downtown to an old, graffiti-strewn neighborhood, not far from Ohio State University's campus.

The day care wasn't large. Or fancy. But it was clean. Had caring, licensed, dedicated personnel and enough bars on the windows to keep the toddlers inside safe.

Two-year-old Jamal was in his classroom, just as he was supposed to be.

"Dwee, Dwee!" he cried, hurrying over to her in a mixture of a plump-thighed run and hurried crawl.

"Hey, little guy!" she said, swinging him up against her for a hug before settling him on her hip. After her meeting with Carrie Woods, she'd needed a reminder of happy endings.

Needed a dose of good to bring back the believing.

"Hi, Sandy," she greeted the slim black woman who followed the toddler over.

"Ms. Lincoln! It's good to see you."

"This little man sure looks healthy," Audrey said, unable to prevent the critical gaze she ran over the child's scalp, ears, over the skin exposed by well-worn but clean shorts and T-shirt. His sandals had a broken strap that had been crudely stitched, but the knots were numerous. And tight.

"He hasn't missed a day since you brought him to us," Sandy said, raising her voice to be heard over the teacher behind her, corralling a group of six or so two-year-olds into a circle for a game of ring-around-the-rosy.

"Posy! Posy!" Jamal said, his little feet pushing against Audrey. Setting him down to join his pals, she smiled, soaking up the joy that happy little body brought.

"His mother drops him off like clockwork every day," Sandy said, her gaze following Audrey's. "And always with this look of relief when she finds out we're still here. All she needed was a chance…"

Yes, Jamal was one of Audrey's successes. A young boy who'd been neglected, left alone, locked in a one-room apartment with nothing but blankets and toys, a couple of filled bottles, while his desperate young mother went out to work to earn money for his diapers and dinner.

A young mother who so obviously loved her son. Recognizing that, taking a chance, Audrey had hooked up the young woman with a couple of social service programs, and now, not only did her son have a safe place to play while she worked, they both had a bed to sleep in, in a bigger apartment, too.

Life wasn't going to be easy for Jamal. Temptations would be numerous in that rough neighborhood, opportunities few. Even so, Audrey gave him an eighty percent chance of success.

He might not have Carrie's opportunities, or Audrey's, either, for that matter, but he had unconditional love. And that was the greatest asset of all.

BY FIVE O'CLOCK Audrey had managed to knock off most of her to-do list for the day—a feat rarely accomplished simply because she had a tendency to keep adding items way after the list was full. Today it didn't seem to matter how many times she weighed herself down, she had enough adrenaline to push back to the top.

She was going to stay one step ahead of last night's phone call if it killed her.

She should have been tired. Beat. Ready to go home, have a cool glass of tea, lie on the daybed on her back porch and fall asleep. And then, maybe, if she roused herself later, she'd put together some kind of salad for dinner and find her way into an old *Law & Order* episode. Or *Without a Trace*.

No, maybe it was a night for *Sex in the City*. Or, not that she'd ever let anyone know she watched it—ever—*Charmed*.

Driving slowly in deference to the Friday-night traffic heading out of the city, Audrey thought about that tea. And the daybed. She tried to feel good about them. To let them call out to her, pull her home.

She thought about television shows and the fiction on her bookshelf.

And in the back of her mind, she fought the same battle she'd been fighting all day. The refusal to think about Ryan Mercedes, or what she'd been doing last Friday night.

Or to allow herself to wonder about the man who'd paid her child support all those years.

She didn't want to think about men at all.

CHAPTER NINE

SWEAT DRIPPING down the middle of his back, he ran through the woods, a wolf behind him, a fugitive in front of him. Tracking them by the sounds of their footsteps in the fallen, crusty leaves covering the ground, making it slippery, Ryan gasped for air. His chest was going to burst. There was a cottage ahead, in the midst of a million acres of one-hundred-year-old leafless trees.

Could he make it inside before the wolf jumped his back? Could he convince the fugitive to join him there? Gun in hand, Ryan knew that he had no time left. One choice was going to save lives—or get him killed.

Just as he reached the side of the cottage, he heard the knocking on the door. Skidding to a halt, he pressed himself against the rough logs that were the side of the building, watching behind him, his gun pointed forward. The knocking came again. Five soft raps. Same as the first time.

It was a trap. The fugitive was there—though Ryan had no idea what he looked like. He and the wolf were partners. Ryan should have known. Should have seen...

Five soft raps. Ryan sat straight up. And blinked—saw himself fully clothed in his own bed, right arm stretched out in front of him as though pointing the gun that was on the night-stand beside him. And realized that someone was at his door.

SHE COULDN'T EXPLAIN why she was there. Ryan was a kid. Kids were full of drama and confidence, and the certainty that whatever was going on in the moment was forever. And they changed course as often as Audrey changed her underwear.

Her daybed was waiting for her. And that glass of tea. What a fool she'd been, thinking of *Bruce Almighty*. And *The Mirror Has Two Faces*. The wine Ryan had brought. His insistence they talk about why she liked that movie.

His reaction to her conversation. Pulling things out of her that no one had ever accessed before.

His even knowing they were there. Caring.

She should never have thought about those things. They were a mirage, calling her to something that didn't exist. Driving her to make turns she didn't want to make, to do things she knew were not right for her.

Just as she'd done nineteen years before. Acting against her better judgment because she needed to be loved.

Turning her back on his unanswered door, not wanting to know who this Friday night's lucky companion was, how old she was, if she'd stay tomorrow night, too, Audrey determined to throw away every single Barbra Streisand movie in her collection. And every Jim Carrey one, too.

As a matter of fact, she wasn't going to watch movies again. Who needed them?

He'd been a virgin, he'd said. Even if she believed that, most particularly if she believed that, she'd have to believe he had a woman in there. A younger woman.

She spun around and knocked one more time.

What man, after tasting the fruits, didn't gorge himself? Especially if he'd waited twenty-two years to take his first taste.

Oh, yes, he'd tasted. All of her. His tongue moving over her skin, leaving a trail of sensation that still made her tingle a week later.

Ryan hadn't loved her as though it was his first time. He'd been gentle, slow, controlled enough that he put her first.

He'd been amaz—

"Audrey? Come in. I... You should have called. I wish you had called. Or at least answered my calls."

She *should* have called. "I woke you up." The short tendrils of his hair were standing on end, his eyes sleepy-looking. Fire swirled in her belly and she wanted to take him right back upstairs to bed.

"No, really, it's okay. I... What time is it?" He glanced behind him as though Delilah were going to appear with the answer.

He'd invited Audrey in, but still stood in the doorway, blocking her way.

"Five-thirty."

Maybe he wasn't alone. Maybe he didn't know what to do with the thirty-five-year-old woman parked on his doorstep.

Her first awkward, other-woman moment.

She could have lived without it.

He raised an arm, his hand going to the back of his neck, showing her the skin beneath his unbuttoned, wrinkled white dress shirt. "Damn, is it really that late?"

Audrey stared. And nodded. That chest. She hadn't been dreaming it to be better than reality all week.

As a matter of fact, her dreams had fallen short.

Sometimes life was just plain cruel.

"I meant to sleep for a few hours is all, so I won't be up all night. Listen, I need a shower. Would you mind putting on a pot of coffee while I go try to wake up? You remember where everything is, right?"

Once again, Audrey nodded. And in spite of the fact that she hadn't said she'd come in and had had no intention of stepping foot over that threshold ever again, she wordlessly followed him inside.

It was only polite to let a man brush his teeth before you blasted him.

IF HE COULD HAVE pulled it off, Ryan would have forgone the shower. As skittish as Audrey was, she might cut out on him as soon as she heard the water running. Best guess, he figured chances were fifty-fifty.

Not good odds, but he took them. He needed to wake up. To wash away the cigarette smoke he'd encountered in the jail cell of the alleged murderer he'd visited the night before.

A bigheaded college fraternity man, a year younger than Ryan. He'd killed his own father. For drug money. Then played Russian roulette with the corpse. There'd been witnesses. Frat brothers. They'd kept score on a legal pad. And been stupid enough to leave it lying on the edge of his father's desk in the study where the man had just written him a check for five thousand dollars.

By the time Ryan got to him, though, the guy had sobered up. He'd had a visit from his mother. Had been crying. Begging.

Ryan had been given the case because they thought he could get a confession out of him.

The whole thing made him sick.

Stripping down, leaving his clothes in a pile on the floor, he stepped into the glass-enclosed shower stall, welcoming the stinging spray of water that was just a little too hot. He needed a few minutes to clean the filth of the world off his skin.

If Audrey left, so be it. He couldn't lock her to his bedpost—though the idea had some merit. He couldn't live his life worried that she was going to jump ship every second.

He couldn't even fully convince himself that he wanted her here. His heart was driving him to be completely one with her—in spite of the obvious obstacles of loving a woman thirteen years older than him.

His head knew he was a loner.

And that he wanted it that way.

So he'd leave it to fate. If she left, she left.

And if she didn't?

He'd learned a thing or two over the past five days of un-answered phone calls. Had grown up, when he'd thought himself all done with that.

He loved Audrey Lincoln. But that didn't mean life was going to be easy. All he had to do was look at Mark and Sara to know that. Now *there* were two people who'd had to face bad odds.

A rapist and his victim? Making it?

Before his mind could take him any further along that confusing path and his own connection to it, Ryan grabbed the soap, rubbing the half-used bar vigorously over his body.

It had been one hell of a long week.

THE SHOWER WAS still running by the time the four-cup pot had dripped its load. And Audrey had paced twice around Ryan's condo, avoiding the picture of the adopted parents who'd raised him. Of him with them.

Avoiding everything that was even remotely personal.

She couldn't look at the couch. That was where she'd first confided in him. Where she'd known that if he kissed her, she'd kiss him back.

The television. Well, that went without saying. Memories of that were what had gotten her into this position tonight to begin with.

She glanced upstairs. Listening. The water was still running. At least he didn't have anyone up there with him.

Tendrils of desire pooled in her pelvis—and below. What was she going to do when he came downstairs? How could she yell at him when, here, in his home, she understood why he'd tried to find her father. He was adopted. Had searched out his birth mother. Though he'd never told her how the search turned out.

Still, she had to tell him to stay out of her business. Even when he meant well. She had to stand up for herself. To make sure she was in charge of her life.

And her choices.

The shower was still on. What was he doing up there?

Tomorrow. She'd call him tomorrow. Tell him to mind his own business from now on. She'd soften the blow with a thank-you for a wonderful twenty-four hours. Tell him to call her if he ever needed anything.

No. She couldn't tell him that.

She'd just say…that she'd be seeing him around. If they ever shared a case again.

Yeah, she couldn't yell at him. They'd be working together again. Paid, attorney-guardian ad litems weren't plentiful in this city. They had to keep this civil. End as friends.

Finding herself out in the kitchen again, staring between the coffee pot and the cupboard that housed the white stoneware cups, Audrey made a decision. She opened the cupboard. Pulled down a cup. Filled it. Put in the two tablespoons of sugar Ryan took in his coffee. She'd leave this for him upstairs so he'd have it when he came out of the shower.

The friendly gesture would soften the blow of her leaving without saying goodbye.

Or even, really, hello.

Then she'd go home, lock her doors, turn off her phone and find her way back to herself.

To the woman she knew herself to be. The woman she wanted to be. The one she'd learned how to cohabitate with in a peaceful manner.

HIS EYES WERE CLOSED. Water streamed over his face and down his chest. Ryan knew he had to move. To turn off the spigot. Use the towel hanging on the hook outside his enclosure. Had to find out if she'd left him.

Again.

But what if she hadn't?

Just like that, the fire lit inside him. She could be down there, in his home, waiting for him.

And so what if she was? She wasn't there for sex. He knew that.

His penis hadn't read the memo.

He heard the click, but its source didn't have time to register before he was processing the spurt of cold air on his butt. His mind, usually on a hair trigger, was working far too slowly.

And then, as the slim arms came around him and naked breasts that were already familiar pressed up against his back, his mind quit working completely.

GOD FORGIVE ME. I know not what I do.

His skin was slick, warm, and her hands couldn't get enough. Running them along his stomach, up over his chest, around his shoulders to his back—and down—Audrey soaked up the man who still hadn't turned around, looked at her, said a word.

What in the hell am I doing?

No answer.

She had no answers at all. To any of this. She was so lonely. So god-awful lonely. She'd like to believe, as she stood naked in the young man's shower, that that was all this was. That her response to Ryan was generic, that of a woman who'd been alone too long. Nothing more.

She'd like to believe that. Tried really hard.

"I've missed you so much." The words were dragged out of her, shoved out of her, from someplace inside that she hadn't accessed all week. "I've never felt like this before. Never needed..."

Hooking her arms around him, her hands coming up over his shoulders from the front, Audrey pressed her face to Ryan's rigid back.

"This has been the hardest week of my life. I can't eat. I can't sleep. I hate being in the home that I love because you aren't there. I hardly know you and you've done something to me, to my heart, that I don't understand."

His arms squeezed against his body, trapping hers.

"It's not right. I can't be with you. I know that. I really believe that. And yet I can't get you out of my mind."

She pushed her pelvis up against his butt and almost cried at the relief of connecting to him again.

Even as she knew that, she was falling prey to her old

ways—making choices that she knew weren't right because she needed to be loved.

"I... Help me out here." He still hadn't said a word. Hadn't turned around.

But he was holding her arms. Not pushing her away.

"I don't know what to do, Ryan." She had a seemingly hopeless problem on her hands.

"Here I am, a grown woman, plenty old enough to know better," she said as much to herself as out loud. "I handle crises that would make most people's blood curdle, and manage to stay calm. It's up to me to find the solutions."

Water ran over his shoulders, splashing her face, plastering her hair against her head, and still she held on, her cheek against his skin.

"I'm thirteen years older than you. And here I am expecting you, a kid, to have some kind of solution for me."

She could feel his heart beating. Hard. Steady. A little rapid. And then she felt him move. Slowly, reaching behind himself to steady her, he turned. His green eyes were vibrant, piercing, as he looked at her through half-lowered lids—as though he were trying to mask much of what was going on inside of him.

That mask drove her further into the cauldron of emotion that was where she lived with Ryan. She didn't want him hiding from her. She needed to know what he was thinking. Feeling.

She needed to know him.

"I've got your answer." His voice was low. Husky. And assured.

"What?" She couldn't hide her tears from him. She was in the fire now. All defenses stripped away.

"Love me," he said. And while there was no mistaking the hardness of his penis against her lower body, there was also no doubt that he hadn't meant those words in a physical sense.

"Let me love you," he continued, swallowing with obvious difficulty.

Fear swarmed her, encased her in a buzzing sound that she couldn't silence. "But—"

"Just love me, Audrey," he said again. Firmly. "Let life take care of itself for a while."

God, he felt good. So good. Warm. Solid. There. Tempted to lay her head against his chest, to bury herself in the safety of his arms and forget the world existed, she looked up at him.

"I can't do that." She forced the words. "I'm not that way. I can't just let go. I see too much of what happens when people don't think ahead. When they don't make good choices. When—"

"And you think I don't?" he interrupted gently. His hands in the small of her back, he held her against him, the water falling over his shoulder to sluice its way between them. "I calculate everything, sweetie, you know that."

It was one of the characteristics that had first drawn her to him. Back when she'd thought he was her age. Or close to it.

"Then—"

"And what I know is that there are always things going on that you can't see. Things right in front of you. The way to deal with them is to acknowledge that they're there, to assess the potential damage, weigh it against the potential gain, to determine what control you have and to not waste energy and effort on things you can't control."

"I'm sure that all makes sense, but—"

"There are times when you have to rely on faith, babe. The trick is to know when. I know that this is one of those times."

"How do you know?"

"Gut feeling. It's never led me wrong before."

She wanted to believe him, but how many befores had there been for him? He was only twenty-two. And, in a biblical sense, had only been a man for a week.

"My first month on the force, as a rookie cop, I made what I thought was going to be a routine traffic stop. Something told me to call in the stop before I ever left my cruiser. And to run for the woods to the left of me. The guy was out of his car before I'd fully braked, and rather than follow him directly, I ran for the woods. Just as I was coming out of a thicket, he was running by. I don't know which of us was more surprised when I flew out of nowhere and tackled the guy. I stayed prone on top of him until help arrived. If I'd stood up, attempted to arrest him, if he'd seen me first, I would have been dead. He was lying on a pistol that was loaded and cocked. Turns out he was not only on America's most wanted, but Canada's, too."

Shivering beneath the hot water, held against the warmth of his skin, Audrey pushed the image of Ryan's body, dead and lifeless, away. So he'd been lucky. Thank God he'd been lucky. Still...

"I trusted a rapist once, too," he said now, his gaze completely serious. And a little guarded.

It was a strange statement.

"And?" she asked, tensing.

"The case was solved."

She was sinking fast. Giving in because she needed him. "This isn't a case."

"I know that."

"My head is screaming at me to go home. I'm going to get hurt. And so are you."

Ryan's gaze was intense, in spite of the water dripping over them. Had she finally convinced him? Was he about to tell her to go then? Or beg her to stay? She waited, afraid of what he'd say. Either way.

"What does your heart tell you?"

He expected an answer. She couldn't give him one. She didn't trust her heart. Hadn't since she was sixteen years old.

"Do you love me, Audrey?"

"It's not as simple as that."

His hands on her sides were gentle, supporting her. "Do you love me?"

"It's not about—"

"Do…you…love…me?"

Why had she come here? Why did life have to be so difficult? Why was she in his shower?

One answer covered all the questions.

"Yes, I love you."

CHAPTER TEN

"YOU SHOULDN'T HAVE looked up my father."

"I know that. I'm sorry."

What a strange night. A strange, out-there, disconnected moment. She'd expected to remain on his doorstep and give him a dressing-down, not to stand naked in the shower in his arms and mention his transgression.

And she'd expected him to defend himself.

"It's a problem I've got," he continued, the caring in his eyes so genuine she couldn't look away. "This tendency to charge ahead and take care of things for the people I care about, without first finding out if they want my help. I'm working on it."

What twenty-two-year-old *talked* that way? Certainly none that she'd known.

For that matter, she couldn't think of any men she'd known who were that in touch with their faults—or sincerely committed to working on them. Granted, she hadn't known a lot of men. And her choices hadn't been the best, but—

"Honey?"

"Yeah?"

"The water's gone cold."

She'd noticed. Sort of. Mostly she was outside herself,

looking down at them in the shower. As though they were a couple. As though he belonged to her.

And she to him.

When she was fifty, he'd be thirty-seven. Young. Virile. Just two years older than she was now.

It wasn't right. Couldn't be. He wasn't hers.

Any thoughts to the contrary were suicide.

"WHERE IS HE?"

A couple of hours had passed since the water turned cold. He'd made love to her—twice—and was now scrambling some eggs for their dinner. They'd talked of nothing but each other since he'd turned off the shower. But Ryan knew immediately what she was talking about.

He'd been on this journey himself. A long time ago.

With some strangely similar results. He wasn't sure how much of that he should share with her.

"Here. In Columbus."

"You're kidding." She looked about eighteen, sitting there at the kitchen table, his rumbled dress shirt hanging halfway down her thighs.

Covering the nudity that he knew was beneath those lucky tails.

Adjusting the basketball shorts he'd pulled on for the trek downstairs, Ryan tried hard to miss the tangled blond hair falling around her face, tried not to think about where that hair had been such a short time before.

He had it bad.

"I'm not kidding," he said, focusing enough to keep his answer vague. If she wanted to know, she'd ask. If not, she had a right to her ignorance.

At times, ignorance truly was bliss. Most particularly, he'd found, when it came to biological fathers.

She jumped up. Headed for the toaster. Pushed a couple of innocent pieces of bread down with a bit more force than necessary.

Ryan waited. Scrambled. Turned down the heat as he reached for the cheese.

He handed her the butter. Withheld the knife. She helped herself to another one as he got the plates.

They were halfway through the meal, sitting at his solid wood round table, before she spoke again.

"Okay." He'd never heard the one word be so definitive. But then, he'd never known anyone like Audrey Lincoln. "Where?"

"German Village."

"Nice part of town." There was no judgment, no detectable emotion at all in the response.

"Yeah."

She took a bite of toast. Pushed eggs around on her plate.

"What's he do?"

Ryan was almost ready for seconds. He hadn't eaten since lunch, sometime in the middle of the previous night.

"He's an engineer."

"A professional."

"Mm-hmm."

"Not some loser deadbeat."

Glancing at her over the rim of his coffee cup, he said, "No." But the word was difficult. His research had been interrupted at a critical point. There were key things he didn't know.

As slowly as he'd ever seen anyone eat, she got a bite of eggs to her mouth, and then inside.

He rose, helped himself to more eggs. Sat. Started in again.

"Is he married?"

"Yes."

"Kids?"

"Two."

She'd ripped off a piece of bread, a bite that he'd hoped would make it to her mouth. Instead, she was rolling it around between her fingers.

"How old?"

My age. He almost said. And stopped himself. Now wasn't the time for reminders.

"Twenty and twenty-three."

Audrey dropped the bread ball, her gaze dead-looking as she stared at him. "Your age."

"Yes."

"I wonder if he reads their letters."

"Don't know."

"Do they live at home?"

"One does. Or at least her address is still listed as his."

"Her."

"Mm-hmm." His plate was empty. He liked it better when he had something to do other than watch her hurt.

"I don't want to know their names."

"Okay."

Her eyes narrowed. "But you know them, don't you?"

"Yes."

"Have you seen him? Them?"

"No." But what he'd found was an omen to Ryan—a sign that he and Audrey were meant to find each other. Some things were just too in your face to be coincidental.

And everyone knew cops didn't like coincidences.

Sitting back, her arms folded across her chest, Audrey jutted out her chin. "Isn't it against code for you to access your resources for private use?"

He looked her straight in the eye. "I was following up on a tip."

"What tip?"

"Mail fraud."

"He's involved in mail fraud?"

"No. You said the letter you sent him was returned unopened. It's possible that he never saw it."

"So you looked him up to ask him."

"I looked him up so you could ask him." And he needed to be there when she did. Just in case.

Springing up, she grabbed his plate so fiercely his fork clanged to the floor, catching him on the foot. She didn't seem to notice. With her plate in hand, as well, she continued to the sink where she proceeded to scrub the paint off his china, or would have if there'd been any paint.

And if he'd had china.

Not that he cared. What he ate from didn't matter. Audrey did.

He left her alone as long as he could—about two minutes—then joined her at the sink, coming up behind her to slide his arms around her middle, holding her lightly against him.

"Forget it, Mercedes. I'm not going to see him."

"Fine." It might be for the best. And once his research was done, once he had an explanation for what he'd found, maybe he'd tell her the whole story. About her father. About his father. And the things they had in common.

"Don't *fine* me. Especially not in that tone of voice. You

don't know everything, you know." He'd received fiercer looks than the one she shot him over her shoulder, but only when he was arresting someone.

"I never claimed to know everything."

"I have no need to meet the man. Don't give a whit about him. I put that past to rest a long time ago."

"And that's why you didn't eat any of your dinner? Because you don't care? That's why my message got you here tonight, in spite of your resolve to stay away?"

That got her. She turned, her eyes still shooting bullets at him. "*You* are what brought me here tonight. Let's make that quite clear. You. Not any need to know anything about the man who was present at my conception. He's a biological, nothing more."

He had her. Not quite in the way he'd hoped his words would deliver her up. This was far better.

"*I* brought you here." He repeated her words.

She blinked. And her cheeks started to turn red.

"It's okay, honey. I'd already figured that out."

"Ryan…"

The tears were back and Ryan knew he'd pushed her enough for now. She needed to be held.

And so did he.

They had a lifetime ahead of them to sort out everything else.

"I HAVE TO GO."

Rousing himself from a state of relaxed dozing, Ryan tightened his hold on the naked woman lying against his chest. "Why?"

"I can't stay here."

"Why not?"

"Ryan—"

"Shh." He put a finger against her lips, having no trouble finding them in the darkness. Awareness of her was instinctive. Something he accepted. "It's late, babe. Go to sleep. Tomorrow's soon enough to tackle the world."

Slowly her body relaxed, growing heavier as she drifted off. Ryan dozed some, slept some, always aware, every single second during that night, of the treasure he held.

"Hey, sleepyhead." The scent of coffee wafted into Audrey's consciousness even before she heard the voice.

"Mmm," she said, squeezing her eyes shut against the world and all its challenges. She was in a cozy, warm, perfect place. A place that smelled of the man she loved.

No.

"I brought you some coffee."

Okay, yes. She loved him. Admitting the fact right out didn't change anything.

"Mmm," she said again, hoping he'd take the hint and go away. Or join her and let her drift back to the security of unconsciousness, where all could be as her mind wished it to be.

The bed dipped and she snuggled in, already on her way back to the inner sanctum.

"It's almost eight."

Time was an intrusion.

The fingers running through her hair were not. They should have been, but they weren't.

"Coffee's getting cold and I know how you like it hot."

Oh, yes. God, yes. She liked it hot. With him. Only with

him. Tendrils of desire spiraled down to her core. And she hadn't even opened her eyes yet!

What was the matter with her? Who was this woman? And who slipped a sex pill into her diet? She'd never, ever wanted sex in the morning before. Or any other time, either. Not the way she wanted it with Ryan.

His fingers moved down to her neck, around her ear and back to her collarbone. If she lay there, pretending to sleep, would he go further? Her nipples tingled in anticipation.

She'd read that the average man had a sexual thought once every three minutes and that the average woman had one three times a day. Somehow in the past couple of months she seemed to have been infected with some kind of testosterone disease.

"I know you're awake."

Not if she didn't move. He couldn't be sure.

"You make a sound when you breathe when you're asleep."

She snored?

Audrey's eyes flew open. Wide-awake, dressed in khaki shorts and a T-shirt that expanded far too nicely across his chest, Ryan sat an inch from her nose, staring down at her.

"I do not!"

"How would you know? You're asleep."

Pushing the hair out of her eyes, she sat up, taking his cup out of his hand for a hearty sip. "I don't, do I?" she asked.

"Don't what?"

"Snore."

"No, you don't snore. I never said you snored. You just make a noise in your throat. Very soft. Kind of like a purr."

If she hadn't been holding a hot cup of coffee, she'd have punched him. "I do not!"

"Yeah, as a matter of fact, you do."

He sounded serious. Peering in his eyes, Audrey waited for the smile that didn't come. "I do?"

"Mm-hmm." He took the cup back, sipped. "It's one of the many things about you that I love."

Tempted to ask what the other things were, Audrey couldn't. She had to think. To get them back on track. She was the eldest here.

"Where's my coffee?"

He held up his cup. "Right here."

"We're sharing?"

"I thought it would be kind of nice."

Nice. He was a kid. What did he know about nice? Sharing a cup of coffee? You had to be a lot older to get that that was nice.

"Who told you that?"

"Delilah." His cat, who'd been out from under the couch only long enough to eat last night. The summer heat was making her lazy.

"No, really, who?"

Frowning, Ryan turned her to face him. "Really? You're serious?"

She nodded.

"No one told me. I just thought it sounded nice. Why? Does it offend you to share a cup with me?"

All this for a coffee cup. Feeling incredibly stupid and awkward for making a mountain out of nothing, Audrey blurted the truth. "Of course not. I think it's nice, too."

Putting the cup to her lips, Ryan helped her take a sip and then, holding it arm's length away, leaned in to rub her nose with his before taking her mouth in a kiss that heated her lips far more than the coffee.

"I think it would also be nice if you met my parents today."

"No way." Even befuddled with his kiss, she got that one immediately right.

"Yes way."

"Forget it, Ryan."

"Can't. It's important."

"Why?"

"This past week has been hell. I don't want to go through another like it. The sooner I make you an official part of my life, the sooner you'll start to feel like you belong."

Audrey felt her age. And his youth. "If only it was that simple."

"Of course it's that simple."

"Ryan, just because you introduce me to your folks doesn't mean that they're going to accept me as a part of your life. And when they don't, it will make even being together like this harder."

"So you want to be together like this?"

"No!" A vision of herself, undressing in his bathroom the night before reminded her of the compelling need she'd felt to be close to him no matter what. She couldn't lie to him. "Yes. I want it. A lot. But that doesn't mean I can have it. I want to win the lottery, too."

"You don't have the winning lottery ticket at the moment. You do have this."

She loved his tenacity—when it was directed at helping kids like Scott Markovich.

"Okay, I'm one of those rare people who love cigarette smoke. But I know if I smoke it'll kill me, so I don't."

Eyes curious, a slight smile on his face, Ryan looked at her. "Did you used to?"

"Yes. Briefly. I liked it too much."

"I can't picture you with a cigarette."

"I can't, either, which is why I don't smoke." She gave him a pointed stare.

"You're saying you can't picture us together."

Smart man. Child. Boy. She was lying naked in his bed. Man. "Right."

"Which only proves my point," he said just when she thought she'd made *her* point once and for all. "You can't picture it because you can't see any way for it to work. You're putting up roadblocks that may or may not exist. Until they are really there, we can't attempt to get around them, we can't know whether or not we *can* get around them."

She wanted to argue. Intended to argue. And couldn't find an argument with him right there, being everything her heart had always wanted. "You have a strange way of looking at the world, Ryan Mercedes."

"I know."

She couldn't fight the whole world. Him. Her. Love.

And she couldn't forget the lessons life had taught her, either.

"Okay, I'll meet your folks. But I want your word that when it's as bad as I know it will be, you'll let me go."

"I can't promise that."

"Ryan…"

"I'm just being honest, sweetie," he said, his fingers brushing lightly against her cheek. "I'm not going to make promises unless I believe I can keep them. Unless I intend to keep them."

The sincerity shining from his eyes almost made her cry again. Even if she trusted her heart, there were too many obstacles. "Oh, Ry, why couldn't you have been born ten years earlier?"

"Because you needed more time to catch up with me."

He grinned and she couldn't help but laugh. She also couldn't help sliding down in the bed as he, once again, took her to a place that was everything life had to offer. Physical. Emotional. And spiritual.

She just wasn't that strong.

CHAPTER ELEVEN

"I CAN'T BELIEVE I agreed to do this."

Trying not to feed off her tension, Ryan, whose hand was interlocked with Audrey's on the console between them, gave it a squeeze. "It's going to be fine," he assured her. And tried to believe it himself.

One way or the other, it would be. Whether he was ready for it or not, understood all the ramifications or not, Audrey was a part of him. His parents were a part of him. They had to meet. There was no other option.

"I should have worn a sundress."

Why? So she could drive him crazy with desire while sitting in his parents' home? Not that the jeans and tank top toned down his desire in any way.

A burlap sack wouldn't have done that.

"You look fine."

"I'm too casual."

"They're casual people, sweetie. My dad's a mail carrier and Mom's been stay-at-home my whole life. Her strongest passion—outside of my father and me—is crocheting."

"I've always wanted to learn how to do that. My mom wasn't into crafty stuff at all."

It was going to be fine. Ryan had to believe that. "I'm sure she'd be happy to teach you."

"We'll see."

"You have to give us a chance, Audrey."

"Why do you think I'm sitting here in this truck?"

Because they loved each other. He just had to keep remembering that.

"YOU HAVE A NICE home."

Harriet Mercedes, gray-haired and dressed in baggy, knee-length shorts and a matching T-shirt, didn't look up from the salad she was tossing. "It's old and tattered."

"It's warm and filled with love."

Turning, her hands dotted with pieces of iceberg lettuce and hanging in front of her, Harriet's plump form looked more heavy with worry than extra weight. "Look, Ms. Lincoln—"

"Please call me Audrey. My mother is and always will be Ms. Lincoln to me."

"Look, Audrey—"

"It's okay, Mrs. Mercedes," Audrey said, stepping forward, wishing the floor would open up and suck her in. "I think I know what you're going to say."

When Ryan went outside with his father to help him change a turn-signal light on the older man's truck, Ryan's mother had asked her along to the kitchen to help her with last-minute touches to the lunch she'd prepared. And then refused to let her do anything.

"And I understand. I really do. I tried to tell Ryan it wasn't going to work. It's inappropriate, this difference in our ages. I know that as well as you do. But trying to convince that son of yours…"

The worried clouds in Harriet's eyes didn't dissipate as Audrey had expected.

"I make my living working with families, trying to hold them together, ferreting out problems and seeking solutions to them. I know relationship dynamics and—"

"Apparently you don't know my son as well as you think you do."

Finished with the salad, Harriet pulled out a platter of sandwiches—turkey, by the look of them. Fresh turkey. Not the store-bought packaged sandwich meat Audrey occasionally had.

"I—"

"Ryan follows his heart," Harriet said. "He always has. From the time he came to us he would not be convinced of something unless he felt the truth in it. The sense of it."

Curious to hear every single one of the stories inherent in the words, Audrey said, "That's one of the things I love most about him."

Somehow it didn't feel wrong to express feelings to Ryan's mother that she rarely came right out and said to him.

Telling him was too dangerous.

"Ryan is with you. He chose to bring you home to meet his family, because he's that certain his relationship with you is right."

Someplace deep inside Audrey, she'd known that. Hoped. But... "Ryan's twenty-two years old. If he's to be believed, I'm the first real love he's had. How can he possibly know that being with me is right for him?"

"He *is* to be believed," Harriet said, still standing with the plate of sandwiches. "That's another thing about my son. He tells the truth. No matter what."

Audrey nodded, wished she dared to take the plate, which

must be growing heavy, from the woman who, thank God, was almost as old as her own mother, over to the table.

"When Ryan was fourteen, the normal adolescent hormonal imbalances and insecurities were heightened by his frustration with his inability to understand himself. He was angry a lot of the time, and growing more and more determined to do something about the things that angered him. Which wouldn't have been so bad, except for the things that made him so mad."

Audrey didn't want to know. And was far too fascinated with the details of her young lover's life. How long did it take two men to change a light bulb? "What things?"

Harriet finally left the still-wrapped sandwiches at the table. "His father tried to get a loan at the bank. We'd gotten behind on our bills and he was trying to consolidate. It was one of those catch-22's. If you've got money, they want to loan it to you, but if you don't, you don't qualify for a loan. Ryan was so furious with what he saw as the unjust treatment of his father that he went on the Internet and God knows where else to find out everything he could about the bank manager. When he found out the man had loaned money to a certain young woman who had no job but lived in a nice condominium and drove a nice car, and who often received visits from the bank manager, he sent an anonymous letter to the president of the bank, telling him so."

"How'd he get all that information?"

"He wouldn't say."

"So what happened?"

"An investigation was done. Apparently the man had a couple of such women on the side, kept for his pleasure. He was fired."

"Was he married?"

"Until this all came out. Had a couple of kids, too. She divorced him and, according to Ryan—he contacted the woman a couple of years ago to apologize for disrupting her life so badly—she got everything, including a nice alimony settlement."

"He went back six years later?"

"Yes. That's Ryan," Harriet said, arms crossed as she watched Audrey. "His sense of right and wrong is non-negotiable and completely drives his actions."

"So did his father get the money?"

"Of course not, we didn't qualify, but according to Ryan, the manager now knew what it was like to be a have-not and perhaps he'd be a little more sympathetic the next time around."

"Wow."

"Yes, well, after that Glen and I decided that perhaps Ryan's anger was in part derived from the fact that he was adopted. We thought maybe he'd be more comfortable with the world around him if he had a better sense of self. We told him that if he wanted to find his birth mother, we'd help him."

"Did he?"

"Yes. And there again, Ryan was Ryan. We found out who she was and expected him to want to make contact, but then he dropped the whole thing. Never mentioned her again. Until last year."

Pulling out a chair at the end of the scarred table, Audrey sat, turning with her arms resting on the back of the chair. "He just met her last year?"

"It's hard to believe it's only been a couple of months over a year." Harriet's voice turned inward, as though she was speaking to herself. And then, as though with renewed purpose, she focused on Audrey again. "Unbeknownst to us, he'd looked her up on the Internet all those years ago and had been keeping track of her. After he joined the police force he had even more tracking abilities available to him. He found out that her husband was having an affair and thought it his duty to tell her so."

While it probably should have, the action didn't shock her.

"How'd that go over?"

"Sara's a delight," Harriet said surprisingly. "She was so thrilled to finally meet the son she'd given up that I think he could have told her she only had six months to live and she'd have found that good news."

Sara. The woman had a name. Had only been in Ryan's life for a year, and he'd mentioned none of this.

But it made his pursuit of her father more understandable.

"How about her husband? I'll bet he wasn't as thrilled."

"I'd guess not, though I've never met him," Harriet said. "She left him and their posh home as soon as she confronted him and he told her the truth. He'd had a long-standing thing with his assistant. Because Sara was willing to just walk away with whatever he agreed to give her, their divorce only took about six weeks."

"But I thought Ryan said his birth mother was married."

"She is. She and Mark just had a baby. Marcus Ryan."

"They named him after Ryan?"

"Why shouldn't they? They're brothers."

"Half brothers."

"No." Harriet shook her head. "Full brothers."

Frowning, Audrey was beginning to hope that changing a turn-signal light took a couple of days. "In a year's time she divorced her husband, married Ryan's dad and had another baby?"

Ryan's mother was still young enough to give birth. Of course, more and more women were having children when well into their forties.

Harriet took glasses out of the cupboard. "That's why it's hard to believe it's only been a year. So much has happened."

"So she knew him all along?"

"No. But that's a story you'll have to get from my son," Harriet said, turning with a glass in each hand. "I've already said far more than I should." She filled the glasses with ice. "Ryan's going to be really angry with me for saying this, but sometimes a mother has to do what she has to do." Her gaze bored into Audrey. "Ryan is going to pursue this relationship with you, Ms. Lincoln."

Harriet's tone had changed.

Nodding, Audrey braced herself.

"He's going to get hurt."

"You think I'm toying with him?"

"No." Ryan's mother set the filled glasses on the table. Went for the other two. "Actually, I don't. I think you really care about him," she said with her back to Audrey as she filled the other two glasses with ice.

"I do." Harriet deserved the truth. "More than I've ever cared about anyone."

Harriet sat. "It's not that I have anything against you," she said, looking Audrey straight in the eye. "I don't. You seem like a lovely woman. With a kind heart."

What did you say to that? Especially with the unspoken *but* hanging in the air between them.

"It's just that…Ryan…he won't look beyond what he believes and feels to be true. He won't care about the challenges in front of you. He's going to charge ahead, regardless of the fact that you and he are a generation apart. And, eventually, as you take him about in your circle, as people raise their eyebrows at the two of you, as he loses a promotion because his superiors doubt the wisdom of his choices, he's going to be hurt."

"I won't hold him back."

"No, I don't think you would. But don't you see, if he's committed to you, made promises to you, his sense of right and wrong will hold him there. Trapped."

Trapped. Oh, God. She could understand. Her love for a young man could stop the progression of his life before it even began. Until his youth was gone and he'd lost opportunity.

Or could it? Was today's world really that small-minded?

"Ryan said you're thirty-five." Harriet spoke again.

In that moment, she sounded ancient. "That's right."

"Sara, his birth mother, is only thirty-eight."

Practically a peer. They'd have been in high school at the same time.

"People are going to think that you're old enough to be his mother."

She'd already gotten that.

"It's off-putting."

She got that, too.

"And what about friends? You going to hang out with Ryan's high-school buddies? They're still in college, having frat parties. Their idea of a family dinner is to stop in at Mom's long enough to wolf down whatever's on the table and head out to party."

Please stop. Oh, please stop.

"Or would you expect him to associate with your crowd all the time? To talk about music and events that took place before he was born? Or when he was too young to be aware of them. What about the Gulf War? I'll bet you remember it."

"Of course I do. I volunteered at the local Red Cross—"

"Ryan doesn't remember it."

"And what about kids? If you don't get started soon, you're going to be too old to have them. Ryan's so young to be strapped with that much responsibility."

And what about when their kids went to school? Had friends over? Would an old mother and young father be an embarrassment to them? Or when they were teenagers and she'd hit fifty and was menopausal and graying and Ryan was a young, virile, thirty-seven, attractive to all the twenty-year-olds, would Ryan and the kids go off and leave her behind to rest?

The idea was only slightly ludicrous, and had a little too much truth for comfort.

"Please," Harriet said, leaning forward. "I don't mean to hurt you, but please, for Ryan's sake, save him from himself."

"You want me to tell him I can't see him anymore."

Tears brimmed Harriet's eyes as she nodded.

The Reader Service — Here's how it works:

If offer card is missing write to: The Harlequin Reader Service, 3010 Walden Ave., P.O. Box 1867, Buffalo NY 14240-1867

NO POSTAGE
NECESSARY
IF MAILED
IN THE
UNITED STATES

BUSINESS REPLY MAIL

FIRST-CLASS MAIL   PERMIT NO. 717   BUFFALO, NY

POSTAGE WILL BE PAID BY ADDRESSEE

HARLEQUIN READER SERVICE
3010 WALDEN AVE
PO BOX 1867
BUFFALO NY 14240-9952

Play the Lucky Hearts Game

and get...
2 FREE BOOKS and
2 FREE MYSTERY GIFTS...
YES! YOURS to KEEP!

I have scratched off the silver card. Please send me my *2 FREE BOOKS* and *2 FREE mystery GIFTS* (gifts are worth about $10). I understand that I am under no obligation to purchase any books as explained on the back of this card.

Scratch Here!
then look below to see what your cards get you...
2 Free Books & 2 Free Mystery Gifts!

336 HDL ESSM   135 HDL ESVX

FIRST NAME   LAST NAME

ADDRESS

APT.#   CITY

STATE/PROV.   ZIP/POSTAL CODE   (H-SR-07/08)

Twenty-one gets you
2 FREE BOOKS and
2 FREE MYSTERY GIFTS!

Twenty gets you
2 FREE BOOKS!

Nineteen gets you
1 FREE BOOK!

TRY AGAIN!

CHAPTER TWELVE

RYAN GOT A CALL HALFWAY through lunch. His commander, head of the Special Victims Unit in the investigative division of the Columbus Police Department, was a man Ryan greatly respected. And one he didn't argue with. He had to go to work.

"Sorry about this," he said as he was backing out of his folks' drive. Before Audrey was even buckled in.

"It's not a problem, Ry." Her voice was distant—as it had been since he'd entered the house with his father. "I understand the demands of your job."

"I'm not usually called in on my days off."

"Did the commander say what happened to Dosendall?" The forty-year-old, fifteen-year veteran was a day-shift special-victims detective whom Audrey had met a few times. He was also a man Ryan trusted.

"Only that he'd responded to a supposed domestic-violence call and ended up shot in the stomach. There's a fifteen-year-old girl involved."

"Which is why he wanted you to come in."

"Right."

Ryan seemed to have a knack for getting the truth out of young people.

"Was anyone else hurt?"

"Not that I know of. I'll be briefed as soon as I get in."

"Do they think the girl shot Dosendall?"

"That's not clear at this time." It was a standard answer. Rote. And all he could give at this point. Even to her.

When silence fell, Ryan started to get a little nervous.

"Overall, that went well back there. Mom seemed to genuinely like you. And Dad was more curious about your job than anything else." Of course, his father rarely gave an opinion the first time out on anything. Glen's way was to listen, watch and then, maybe, say something. Mostly he was there for the aftermath, either to celebrate or help pick up the pieces.

"Mm-hmm."

"Talk to me."

"I am."

Ryan reached for her hand, and when she didn't accommodate his reach, leaned farther over until he could capture it. He held it lightly, half expecting her to pull away and relaxing a tad when she didn't.

"Your mother is my age."

"My mother is fifty-four."

"Your biological mother."

Stopping at a light, Ryan stared straight ahead. Processed. Harriet was not one to speak out of turn. Or to tell others' business. But she had. Things were worse than he'd thought.

He'd misjudged. And Audrey had obviously been hurt.

Damn. Now was not the time to get lazy. Audrey wasn't a case. She was life.

"She's three years older than you are," he said slowly, carefully, until he knew how much she'd been told.

And why.

"We were in high school at the same time."

Ryan's skin grew tight. His mother had talked about Sara's high-school years?

"And?"

"It's not going to work, Ryan. I am your mother's peer, not yours."

"Funny, we were pretty good peers last week when we handled the Markovich case."

"That's different."

"How so? I can work side by side with you, sharing the same amounts of responsibility and workload, but I can't love you?"

"Ryan, please. Not again."

"No. Sorry. I can't give on this one."

"And how much am I going to matter when I'm in my fifties and you're still in your thirties, being hit on by women half my age?"

"As much as you matter right now."

"You're too young to know what you're talking about."

"I've lived long enough to have heard of a lot of men in their forties, fifties and sixties who leave wives younger than they are for women half their age. It's a measure of the man, Audrey, not the age."

At her silence, he continued, "If you're going to argue, please keep the points pertinent. My actions are pertinent. The choices I make are pertinent. The way I treat you is pertinent. The number of years I've been on this earth is not. There are people in their sixties who are less mature than I am."

He could name a couple they both knew, but they only had about ten minutes left together. He couldn't leave her this way. He might not get another chance.

"Why didn't you tell me that you just met your birth mother last year?"

"What does it matter when I met her?"

"That's a pretty big occurrence in anyone's life, Ryan. A defining moment. The fact that you don't talk about it makes me nervous. You say you're all into us, yet you don't give me key pieces of your life."

She had him there.

And he wanted her.

Taking a deep breath, trying not to think about what he was doing, only why, Ryan said, "I have…issues there."

"Obviously. So why don't you want me to know about them? Because you like being her little boy and—"

"Shut up!" Anger with Audrey was a new experience and caught him unawares. "I apologize for that."

"Apology accepted. I was lashing out."

Giving himself a couple of seconds to calm down, he finally said, "My issue isn't with Sara. As a matter of fact, I visit there at least once a week. More if I can. I was there this week, babysitting so she could get a few hours away. She just had a baby and hasn't really left him since he was born, but she agreed to leave him with me."

"Marcus Ryan. Your mother told me about him."

And had she told Audrey about Marcus Ryan's father, too? Chilling, he reminded himself how much he loved Harriet Mercedes. How good she'd been to him. He'd have a talk with her, but not until he could do so without anger.

"She said he's your brother. Your full brother. Not half."

Damn it to hell. He was a grown man. Not a boy, to be talked about by his mommy behind his back. What in the hell had his mother been thinking?

"That's correct."

"Your mother married your father. After all these years."

"That's right."

"Is that your issue, then? The fact that they got together for this baby, but couldn't make it to give you a solid home life? You have problems because they gave you up for adoption?"

What the crap? "What did my mother tell you about Mark?"

"Nothing. She said it was up to you to tell me what you wanted me to know."

Harriet's mental image grew a little clearer in the haze that had been blinding him.

"I don't blame Sara for giving me up for adoption," he said, stopping at the light around the corner from his house. "She was sixteen, a child. There was no way she could have given me a solid home life even if she'd wanted to."

"I get that."

He turned. His complex's driveway was ahead. Her car right around the corner, in guest parking.

"My issue is with Mark."

"Did he desert her? Leave her alone and pregnant?"

"He didn't even know she *was* pregnant."

He'd stopped the car. Rather than immediately jumping out, Audrey turned to him. "Well, then, how can you blame—"

"He didn't know because he was in prison."

AUDREY WAS WASTING her time. Had no need to see anyone—especially someone she'd never met. She'd rescheduled Saturday's appointments to meet Ryan's parents and now had time on her hands. Thinking to do.

And since she always thought better when she drove, she was driving.

German Village wasn't as far as she sometimes drove when she had an issue to resolve, a challenge to face. Only twenty minutes from her own little house in the northern part of the city, the quaint German neighborhood was one of those places she'd heard of, but never really visited. If she didn't have a client there, she didn't get there.

Most of Audrey's clients weren't from the affluent, renovated historic neighborhood with its cobblestone streets, big homes and upscale coffee shops and eateries.

She'd read about the village. Had always wanted to see it. Why not today? Why not stop for coffee at Cup O' Joe's? She'd never tasted the homegrown Columbus beans served there. Today they seemed like just the distraction she needed.

Perhaps they'd clear her head, wipe away the Ryan-induced fog so she could find some solutions.

Or rather, find a way to enforce the solutions. Staying away from Ryan Mercedes was the answer. That she already knew. How to ensure that she did that, how to get him to stop contacting her, was the issue at hand.

She had no other missive. Nothing else to find. The road away from Ryan was it.

Which didn't explain why, as soon as she had an iced coffee in hand, she was seeking out a phone book from the clerk. Leafing through the Ws, stopping at Wilson. Going down the alphabet until she was at the Ls. Looking for Leonard.

And jotting down the address listed there. She might not be a star detective or have state-of-the-art investigative tools at her disposal, but she could look up a name.

And after half an hour of driving in circles, find a street.

She wasn't going to stop. She'd said so before getting on

the highway downtown. But no one would know if she drove by the house. Took a peek.

Got a measure of the man who'd deserted her.

Ryan's father was an ex-con. It explained so much. And nothing at all.

With a crime scene waiting, he'd been unable to dally, even for a second when they'd reached her car. Or rather, been unable to take time, other than for the very long, thorough kiss he'd given her as he'd come around to walk her to her car and open the door for her.

She hadn't meant to kiss him back. Had been adamantly opposed to the action.

It had happened, anyway.

As had the thoughts that had continually turned to him during her drive. What had his father done? Why couldn't Ryan talk about it? How did it affect him, knowing that an ex-convict had contributed to his genetic makeup? To someone like Ryan, with his rigid sense of right and wrong, his determination to right wrong at any cost, the knowledge had to have delivered a hard blow.

Luckily she was old enough not to be affected by whatever her father had turned out to be. After all those years at the hands of her mother's emotional blackmail, her attempts at brainwashing, Audrey had a clear sense of self.

One that was impervious to a bit of biological information.

She'd prove it, too. She'd find the house. She wasn't afraid to find out that her father's was the only unkempt place in this beautiful neighborhood. The only one with shaggy grass where the others all had sprawling acreage of vivid green lawns that looked as though they'd be as soft as cotton on the bare feet of the children who ran there.

The end of the street came before she found the ramshackle home she'd been searching for. No matter. She had time. Could turn around.

The house numbers were all in order—and clearly marked. Following them wasn't a problem. Nor did it take long to find the house that matched the address she had.

It was the one with the distinguished-looking gentleman operating an edge trimmer on one of the immaculate lawns.

She backed up. Turned. Coasted past the drive. He was in designer denim shorts and a white polo shirt.

Her foot slipped off the gas. She was staring. And couldn't make herself leave.

"Can I help you?"

The man was beside her, calling loudly enough for her to hear from inside her car.

"Are you in trouble?" He grabbed his cell phone. "I can call 9-1-1."

"No!" She hadn't meant to say that quite so loudly. Or sharply. But 9-1-1 connected, indirectly, to Ryan. She didn't want him to know anything about this foray into insanity. Ever. Rolling down her window, she said, "I'm fine, really. I was lost, but now I've figured out where I am."

In more ways than one.

"I'm Leonard Wilson," the damn man said, holding out a hand to her. "My wife's inside. Why don't you come in and have some tea? We can look up your destination on the computer, help you find your way. A young woman shouldn't be lost and alone in downtown Columbus."

Tell me about it, you jerk. "Maybe if you hadn't deserted her, left her alone with a lunatic woman all her life, she wouldn't be."

Where on earth that comment had come from, Audrey had no idea. It shocked her far more than it did the gaping man staring at her.

"What?"

She'd started it. "You heard me."

"I deserted you?"

"That's what I said."

He paled. "Audrey?"

Inexplicably, her name on his lips changed everything, drained her anger. Left her numb. "I'm sorry," she said more softly. "I have the wrong address," she stumbled over the words. She couldn't believe she'd done this.

Done any of the things that she'd done in the past two weeks. Things such as going to bed with a twenty-two-year-old kid. Falling in love with him.

She was her mother, after all. Out of her ever-loving mind.

"It's you, isn't it?" Leonard Wilson was leaning on her door. In the way of her escape. If admitting her name bought her her freedom then…

She nodded.

"My God." The wide-eyed look on his face wasn't all that complimentary, though she couldn't determine, in her addled state, if it stemmed from horror or sheer shock. "For years I prepared for this moment, but when your teens passed, and then your twenties, I assumed the day would never come."

She wasn't falling for any sob story. Any attempt at convincing her that he'd cared at all. Audrey was a pro at withstanding parental manipulation.

"Yes, well, it didn't. As I said, I'm lost—"

"On my street? In front of my house? Wouldn't you say that's a bit much to be a coincidence?"

"Len? Who is it, dear?"

Looking up, Audrey saw the fiftyish, smartly dressed woman walking toward them. Her voice sounded kind. A lot kinder than Audrey's mother's. Her expression was softer, too.

"You're never going to believe this," Leonard said, still holding the door as though he knew that if he let it go, Audrey would be gone.

Why on earth should he care?

"It's not as if I live a thousand miles away," she told the man she hated almost as much as she wanted to know him.

"It's Audrey," he said, putting an arm around the woman who came to join him.

Audrey wasn't sure he'd heard her statement. Hardly remembered it herself as she stared at the woman who'd joined them. She'd never seen her in her life, but the woman peering at her had tears in her eyes.

"Do I know you?"

"This is my wife, Becky," Leonard's words seemed to come from far away.

Audrey glanced at Leonard. "What's going on? Do I know her?"

"No, honey, you don't." Leonard shifted, taking much of his wife's weight. "But I think you should come in. We've got some things to tell you."

"I've lived in Columbus my entire life."

"And if we had contacted you, we'd have gone to jail."

CHAPTER THIRTEEN

THE GIRL HAD obviously been penetrated according to the doctor's report Ryan had just taken. Standing outside the hospital room, at the same hospital where he'd just seen the wife of one his associates waiting while her husband underwent surgery for the bullet in his gut, Ryan took a deep breath before nodding at the female police officer, Kelly Jones, that he was ready to go in.

Takeisha Baker looked more like ten than fifteen, her tiny figure seemingly swallowed up by the bars of the bed pulled up around her. The bruises weren't easily detectable on her dark skin, but the swelling around her eye was unmistakable. As were the tears that sprang to her eyes when she saw them.

Though she didn't say a word, her lips were trembling, as though there were many things she wanted to say. Or needed to say.

"Hi, Takeisha, I'm Detective Mercedes and this is Officer Jones."

"I didn't do it." The girl's voice was strong, solid. "I swear I didn't do it."

"Do what?" Ryan pulled up a chair a couple of feet from the side of the bed and sat. Much less intimidating to the girl than having someone standing over her. Especially a man.

"Shoot that cop. I didn't do it."

"We're not here to talk about that right now," he said, though he desperately needed to find out what the girl knew. Needed to avenge his brother officer—and the family that paced, fearing the worst, a couple of floors below. "We're here for you."

Takeisha frowned, her gaze dropping. She didn't look convinced. "He says it's my fault," she half muttered. "Probably it is."

"What's your fault?"

"What he did. What he's been doing."

"Who?"

"Daniel."

"Who's Daniel?"

"My old lady's man. He's been living with us awhile now."

"And what did he do?" Ryan knew. Kelly knew. There was no reason to put the child through this, except to protect her. They needed official testimony to press charges.

"He's been making me do it with him, trying to get me pregnant."

Exchanging a glance with Kelly, who was holding the tape recorder, Ryan sat forward. "Trying to make you get pregnant?" They'd get a little clearer testimony on the rest of it in a minute.

"Uh-huh. My ma can't have any more kids. Something inside her busted with the last one."

"So they want you to be a surrogate mother?"

"What?" Takeisha's eyebrows drew together.

"They want you to have their baby for them," he re-stated. Shaking her head, flipping the tiny braids covering it,

Takeisha snorted. "They don't want a baby. They want more money on the welfare check. You get so much for every kid."

It was a good thing he'd only had a few bites of lunch before he'd been called away. Ryan had seen a lot in his few years on the force, heard some horrendous things, but somehow, sitting in the presence of a fifteen-year-old child who had far too much maturity and bore the marks of gross sexual impositions, was one of the hardest things he'd ever done.

"So he made you have sex with him." Kelly's voice brought him out of his stupor and back to the job at hand.

"Yeah."

"And how long has this been going on?" It was Kelly again.

"I don't know. Four months, maybe."

"Did you tell the doctor about that?"

"Yeah. She did a pregnancy test."

Ryan wanted to kill the bastard who'd made his mark on this child—and prayed that the test came up negative. What in the hell was the matter with people? With the world?

"Can you tell us what happened today?" he asked, managing to fill his tone with the emotional calm he couldn't find inside himself.

"We were sitting there watching cartoons and Daniel said he wanted it and my ma said no. She said he'd done it enough to make me pregnant and he had to stick with her now. He got mad and said he'd have it with me whenever he wanted. He said that I was his now, too. He said he'd show her."

The girl's voice broke and her face folded as she started to cry. "He grabbed me and…he…while he was doing it, she came in with a gun. He jumped up and they started fighting and I was afraid he was gonna kill her, so I called 9-1-1."

There had been mixed stories about who'd actually made that call—the mother or the daughter.

"Then what happened?"

"He heard what I did and he slapped me." She touched her eye. "My ma hit him with the gun and he grabbed her arm that was holding it and just as that cop came in the gun went off."

"Did anyone actually point the gun at Officer Dosendall?"

"Uh-uh." Takeisha looked them straight in the eye. "They were so busy fighting they didn't even know he'd gotten there."

The shooting had been an accident. A man might die, a great cop might die, and it had been accident.

They'd still get this Daniel guy. And maybe the girl's mother, too, though he doubted that. They'd give her immunity in exchange for her testimony.

And with that testimony, they'd probably win. They'd get him for rape. And manslaughter. Give him ten to twenty years in prison.

Ryan had been hoping for first degree attempted murder. And, if it didn't mean Dosendall had to die first, the death sentence.

"I'M SORRY, I don't mean to stare, but I just can't believe I'm actually looking at you after all this time," Becky Wilson said. They were sitting in the Wilsons' living room, the older couple so close they were touching on the off-white leather couch, Audrey in a matching, oversize chair.

Sipping from the sweet tea Becky had brought, Audrey didn't respond. These people were acting as though she'd returned from another planet when, in fact, they'd lived in the same city for most of her life.

Still…

"What did you mean when you said if you contacted me, you'd go to jail?"

Leonard Wilson was perfectly fine-looking. Short-haired, slim, slightly muscular, with a distinguished air that commanded Audrey's respect even when she wanted to hurl insults at him. He had green eyes. And didn't look as though he'd ever been blond. His eyebrows were too dark. He was easily six-two.

As long as she'd waited for her legs to grow, she'd never been particularly tall.

As a matter of fact, she couldn't find even a hint of resemblance between her and the man sitting there watching her with compassion-filled eyes.

"It's hard to know where to begin," he said.

"I always find that the beginning is a good spot."

The response was more sardonic than snotty, but she'd come close to disappointing herself with a childish display.

But then, how appropriate, since she was this man's child.

How could he be so calm about all this? He should be stammering with guilt. At the very least.

"You're right, I'm sure," he said with a small grin. "I was very much in love with your mother when I married her."

Amanda did seem to attract people like magnets. Until they got to know her intimately. She had more loyal business associates than Audrey could count.

"She's a beautiful woman," Audrey offered, wiping condensation from her glass on her jeans.

"And smart and funny," he added. "When she wants to be."

"My brother said the same things about her," Becky said, her cheeks not as white and colorless as they'd been moments before.

Audrey's brow creased. "Your brother."

"He was everything your mother was not," Leonard said. "Artistic, spontaneous. He was a designer, mostly women's leather goods, but he had a line of clothes, too."

Because she suddenly needed to stall this story, Audrey asked Becky, "Is he someone I'd have heard of?" She'd worked with her mother in the stores for several years.

"No, but if he'd lived, he would have been. He'd just sold his first line to all the major houses in New York when he was killed, flying his two-seater home to Ohio. He'd taken off in bad weather…" Becky's voice fell off.

"He was hurrying home to see your mother." Leonard confirmed what Audrey had been half-expecting, half-dreading she'd hear.

"She was having an affair with him."

"Right."

She peered at Leonard. "While she was married to you."

"Yes."

"Did you know about him?"

"I'd just found out. Which was why Jeff was hurrying home to her."

Sweating, Audrey sized up the two of them, the linked hands, the love that was evident between them even after more than twenty years of marriage. And she could fill in some of the blanks.

Just not the crucial one.

She wasn't sure she wanted to know. Not now, when she'd finally brought herself here, when she'd finally acknowledged that she had to have contact with the man who'd fathered her.

"Your mother and I had been having problems. My fault,

in that I'd started to pull away from her. She always needed a lot of attention and reassurance that she was loved and I was fine with that. It was the instances of verbal and emotional cruelty and manipulation I couldn't stand. As time wore on, I started distancing myself emotionally just to survive. And the more I did that, the more abusive she became. When she told me she was pregnant, I was surprised as we'd used birth control. But I thought this was a sign that we were meant to be together and I opened my heart to her again, thinking that the child—you—would give her the emotional confidence she needed to overcome the outbursts."

So Leonard *was* her father.

As the older man paused, Becky's hand in his moved, as though she was giving his fingers a squeeze.

"I told her I wanted us to go to counseling, that with a baby on the way, I was insisting on counseling so that she wouldn't bring to you whatever problems she brought to the marriage. I wanted her happy. I wanted us all happy."

Audrey could understand that. She would have made a similar recommendation had she been called in as mediator to a home life such as Leonard described.

She wanted to hate the man—or at least resent him. Sympathizing with him, she was having a little trouble doing either.

"The request must have scared her," Leonard said, his gaze turned inward as he shook his head. "I can only guess that she was afraid someone might find something seriously wrong with her. She went off on me like she'd never gone off before. She kept telling me that if she was crazy, it was my fault. All she'd wanted was to be loved and I didn't love her."

Audrey chilled at the familiar words, only vaguely aware

that she was clutching her glass of tea the way she used to clutch her teddy bear—in front of her for protection.

"The more I tried to calm her, to assure her that I only wanted what was best for all three of us, to assure her that I would stand beside her, help her, support her no matter what was discovered, the more out of control she got," Leonard continued, his voice gaining strength as he told his story.

"And when, no matter how cruel she got, I wouldn't give in to her as I usually did, she told me that the baby wasn't mine."

"She was just lashing out," Audrey said.

"I thought so, too, except that she'd calmed as she'd said the words. There was fear in her eyes, but something else, too. Suddenly her whole demeanor changed and she told me about Jeff. About the affair they'd been having for more than six months."

"So you left." Audrey didn't blame him. She wasn't his. His wife had been unfaithful.

"I wanted to leave. I told her I was leaving. And then Jeff was killed and she was alone and pregnant and falling apart."

"She said you were divorced before I was a year old."

"She wouldn't let me touch her. Said that would be unfaithful to Jeff. As the months wore on, she wouldn't let me near her at all. I'd met Becky at Jeff's funeral—yes, I went with your mother to her lover's funeral because I was afraid she'd fall apart and there would be no one there to help her—and Becky had asked to be kept apprised of the pregnancy and your particulars. You were her only sibling's child and she so desperately wanted to know you."

"I would think my mom would have welcomed Jeff's sister into the fold."

"She caught us talking one time and wouldn't let Becky anywhere near. I'm sure she was afraid that Becky and I had something going, or would have. She was afraid that I'd leave her."

"Even though she so obviously didn't want you." Knowing her mother, the picture was becoming so crystal clear.

"Eventually it got so bad that she changed the locks on the doors. She was convinced that Becky and I were having an affair—which, at that point, we were not. I came home to find that I couldn't get in my own house."

Audrey would like to have been surprised.

"A week later she filed for divorce."

"Before I was born."

"Yes."

"But she still named you on the birth certificate."

"I suspect that was to punish me. To make me pay child support. I'd just started my own engineering firm and she knew that I was scraping every penny to get by."

Audrey suspected he was right.

"You could have fought that."

"I know."

The things Leonard left unsaid, as he and Becky watched her with expressions full of love, hurt even as they promised miracles to come.

She had a family.

"She robbed us of a lifetime."

She heard her words speaking about her mother, and felt sick to her stomach as she saw herself, as well. Had she been so busy trying to control her world, to prevent further pain, to keep others from hurting her, that she was robbing herself of a lifetime?

RYAN CALLED Audrey on his way from the hospital to his office. He'd stopped by to check up on Dosendall's wife again. There was still no word about the officer's condition.

And there was no word from Audrey, either. No voice-mails. No text messages, not that she'd ever sent him any. And she didn't pick up her phone.

With lead in his gut, afraid that his mother had scared her off again, that another long week of unanswered calls was going to follow, he dialed his parents' home.

"I love her, Ma," was the first thing out of his mouth when his mother picked up.

"I know you do, Ry."

"I want you to stay out of it."

"You're going to get hurt."

"Since when have you thought you could prevent that?" Silence followed his remark.

"You hurt her," he said.

"I didn't mean to, son, but I've told your father about our conversation and have been worried about how she left here feeling. I've never in my life let someone leave my home feeling unwelcome."

"You didn't pick a great time to start." The intake of breath on the other line, along with the words still ringing in his own ears, showed him his cruelty. "I'm sorry. That was uncalled for."

"I'll call her, Ry."

"No! Please. Just leave her alone. I'll take care of it. I only need to know what you told her."

His heart didn't feel any lighter when, five minutes later, he hung up the phone.

"I CAME HERE thinking I'd find a deadbeat father and, instead, I find out that my father has been dead since before I was born," Audrey said, trying to assimilate the cacophony of emotions assailing her as she stared at the couple across from her.

Their home was cool in the middle of a hot summer. Yet warm, too.

"But you found an aunt who's desperately wanted to be a part of your life since before you were born," Leonard said softly.

Audrey's heart started to pound as she glanced at the other woman, read the anticipation and barely concealed emotion in her eyes, in the trembling of her lips.

"I—I didn't get that far in my thinking yet," she allowed. "I mean, my father is more than a name now. The fact that he has family never even occurred to me."

And something else dawned.

"What about your mom and dad? Are they alive?" Did she have grandparents somewhere?

"No. They passed away when I was seventeen. In a car accident. Jeff was only twenty-three at the time, but he'd already graduated with a degree in design and was apprenticing with a house in New York. I finished high school there with him, then came back to Ohio State to attend college with my best friend. When he'd established himself enough to be making a living from his own designs, he moved back to town, too."

A photo on the mantel caught Audrey's attention. A photo she'd purposely avoided upon entering the room. "I have cousins."

"Yes, Carla and Kaylee, and they know all about you," Leonard said. "From the time they were little they heard about cousin Audrey. We'd so hoped you'd get in touch with us, and had them prepared for the eventuality."

Her heart plummeted. For a few minutes there, caught up in the wonder—and shock—of it all, she'd forgotten thirty-five years of abandonment. And a letter that was never even read.

"I did get in touch." Audrey forced the words into the loving atmosphere. She was here to face the truth, not to be wrapped in loving-family dreams. "When I was in high school, I wrote you a letter. My mom even gave me your address. I mailed the letter myself. The letter came back, canceled, unopened with 'return to sender' scrawled across the front of it."

Becky's jaw dropped open. "We never received a letter."

Audrey looked at Leonard.

"We absolutely never received a letter," he said. "We'd have been all over it, I can assure you. Every single Thanksgiving since Becky and I were married, there's been a prayer offered at the dinner table that you'd find us."

"It was sent to a Dayton address."

"We've never lived outside of Columbus city limits."

"What about the support checks? They came from all over the country."

"There were no checks," Leonard said. "I paid child services, and they paid your mother."

"Surely she…" Audrey wasn't sure why she was surprised. Amanda's need for control was so complete, so total, she'd go to any lengths to preserve it. Except, maybe, breaking the law. Maybe.

"My guess is she told someone at work a sob story about protecting you and gave you their address. Thinking they were helping, he or she wrote return to sender on your letter and put it back in the mail."

It sounded sickeningly like something Amanda Lincoln could do.

Still…

"I was right here in town. You could have contacted me."

Leonard leaned forward. "After I left your mother she swore she'd make Becky and me pay for the rest of our lives for hurting her. She called the police on me when I stopped by the house to pick up some of my things. She called and reported my car as stolen. Her name was on the title. Mine was on the title of the car she'd said she wanted and was driving. I was arrested that time, but the charges were dropped. Then she really started to play dirty."

Leonard looked away, out the window, before meeting Audrey's gaze again. Becky rubbed his back. "When I was first in love with your mother, when I thought I'd found my life's mate, I poured out my soul to her. Because I wanted her to know me completely, I told her all my dark secrets and indiscretions. With the blindness and confidence of young love, I trusted her to keep them sacred. Systematically, throughout the years, she used them all against me. Except one."

Elbows on his knees, Leonard said, "When I was eighteen I had sexual relations with my girlfriend. We'd been going together for a couple of years, but she was only sixteen at the time. Her father pressed charges and I was found guilty of statutory rape."

"You went to prison?" Considering the quiet dignity, the

soft speech of the man sitting with her in his well-to-do living room, the thought of him housed with hard-core sexual offenders was difficult to imagine.

"I went to jail for the few months it took to have a trial and sentencing. Because I was only eighteen and the sex was consensual, the judge was able to give me a suspended sentence and a monetary fine."

Audrey had no reason to feel relieved. This man was nothing to her except her mother's ex-husband.

"Your mother ran into one of our friends at the grocery store shortly after the car incident and happened to bring the conversation around to rape—mine in particular. This friend was also a business associate of mine."

"And you couldn't get her for slander because she spoke the truth."

"Right. I went to her, begging her to let it go, reminding her that she hadn't been happy with me, appealing to her on Becky's behalf, for Jeff's sake. That got to her. Sort of. She said that we'd have complete peace from her if we signed a contract agreeing that we would not contact you, ever, either directly or indirectly, by any means. She said that was the only way she'd feel assured that I would not be popping in and out of her life. She wanted to never see Becky or me again." He shook his head.

"At first he point-blank refused." Becky took over the story. "I insisted we get a lawyer and that's when we found we had no rights whatsoever where you were concerned. Your mother could prove that Len wasn't your biological father. At that time we didn't know she was planning to name him on the birth certificate or come after him for child support. In those days extended families, an aunt, had even fewer rights than they do now. So we weren't going to see you, anyway."

"I hated to leave you alone with her," her uncle inserted. "But we didn't have enough grounds to have her proved unfit. She had a respectable job, employees who would vouch for her. You weren't even born yet and the courts almost always placed children with their mothers in those days, anyway."

"We talked," Becky nodded toward Leonard, sliding her hand along his leg. "And we figured that you had the best shot of her being a good mother to you if we bowed out. But at our lawyer's suggestion, we did get your mother to add a caveat to the contract. If you ever contacted us, we could see you."

"So she made sure I didn't contact you," Audrey said now, the whole thing making sense. Horrific sense, but sense. "She was afraid she'd have had to share me with your family—a family she couldn't be a part of."

"Probably." Leonard's smile was sad.

"Regardless," Becky said, her lips trembling again, "we signed the contract, but have prayed every year since that you would come to us."

So much pain. Heartbreak. Loneliness. For all of them. All because one woman feared them. Amanda Lincoln, in trying to control what couldn't be controlled—the heart— had brought emotional agony to everyone who had loved her. Including herself.

Somehow, the cycle had to stop.

CHAPTER FOURTEEN

SHE DIDN'T ANSWER her phone. Or return his calls. Ryan thought about the advisability of giving her a day to recover from the meeting with his mother, wondered if it was the mature thing to do.

And as soon as he was finished at work, he presented himself outside Audrey's front door, knocking with the confidence of one driven by instinct, not head trips. He was who he was—a man who did what he felt to be right. If that made him young, so be it. He guessed, if that was the case, he'd still be as young at eighty-two as he was at twenty-two.

A new youth serum. He could market it. Make a million.

And didn't believe for a second that Audrey Lincoln would be any more swayed by him as a millionaire than she was with him as an underpaid detective.

It wasn't his job that bothered her. And she wasn't the kind of woman who could be bought.

By the third knock he was shifting his weight from foot to foot, stewing. He couldn't harass her. That was against the law. He couldn't break in. That was against the law.

Unless he had a search warrant.

Which he did not.

Dialing her cell again as he stood there on her front porch, he counted the rings. It was almost eight o'clock. Where in the hell was she?

He could get a search warrant easily enough. All he had to do was claim that she was a woman living alone—a woman who dealt with some pretty rough characters in her line of work. He could...

Was she really just going to refuse to see him? To give them a chance?

He could write a letter. Leave it in her door.

And write more. And leave them again and again for as long as it took to get her to talk to him.

Thoughts of how it would look for a detective to have a civil stalking order against him were just surfacing when he saw Audrey's car come up her street. Half expecting her to drive right on past when she recognized his car at the curb, he had to concentrate to quiet the pounding of his heart when she pulled into the drive.

"Hi." She wasn't frowning as she approached him, still in the jeans and tank top she'd had on that morning, her purse slung casually over her shoulder.

"Hi."

"Would you like to come in?"

Hell, yes, he would. Of course he would. There was nothing he'd like better. "Okay."

Ryan had never actually been inside Audrey's home. Inside her body, but not her home. Feeling kind of awkward, he stepped into the Victorian-style cottage, with its real hardwood floors, coordinated yellow and green walls, matching furniture and a flat, big-screen television set.

The place, compared to his bachelor apartment, made him feel about twelve.

"It's nice." He looked around—at the wall decor that ranged from what appeared to be real art to shadow boxes and filigree shelf things filled with expensive-looking collections.

"I like it."

"How long have you been here?"

"Five years."

"All through law school?" He wanted to be impressed, not depressed.

"Yeah. I got a thirty-year, fixed-rate mortgage when the rates were low. The payment was less than the rent I was paying on my apartment."

He chose not to share the fact that he hadn't been old enough to qualify for a loan on his own when the rates had been at an all-time low four years before.

She offered him a drink. He wanted lemonade and asked for a beer. With her glass of lemonade in hand, she led him through the fully equipped and immaculate kitchen to an enclosed porch with a rounded back wall of screened windows and tightly woven wicker furniture. A couch, a love seat, rockers, end and coffee tables. There was no new discount-store patio furniture here.

"Where were you?" Cringing at the abruptness in his tone, Ryan dropped onto one end of the wicker couch. He felt awkward as hell and hated it. He sipped his beer, uncharacteristically aware of his youth. Then she sat beside him and his gaze was captured by those brown eyes, which gave him glimpses of some deep, nonverbal communication that he instinctively knew was a once-in-a-lifetime experience.

"Out driving."

There was more. But he didn't ask.

"I went to German Village."

She'd pursued his lead. He'd had a hunch that Audrey had ancient history to settle before she could trust a man with her heart. Any man.

So maybe Ryan had a chance. He leaned his shoulder against hers.

"How'd it go?" He forced calm professionalism when, in fact, he'd have given his right arm to have been there with her.

"He's not my father."

Ryan's eyes narrowed as he watched her, looked for signs of prevarication or hiding. Of residual turmoil.

She seemed strangely at peace.

Nothing at all like he'd felt after meeting his biological mother the year before.

"Did he tell you that?"

Audrey's lips tilted into a soft, half smile that was filled as much with sadness as joy. "He did. And his wife, my aunt, did, too."

Loving the sound of her voice, the look in her eyes, Ryan listened as she told him the story she'd heard that afternoon. And wanted to meet the man who hadn't fathered the woman he loved, but who'd financially supported her, anyway—the man who'd told her the whole truth, sparing himself nothing.

"How'd you feel about him then?" He stopped her when she got to the part about Leonard having been convicted of raping a minor.

"She was his girlfriend," Audrey said. "It was completely consensual. They made love. Her father found out and went berserk."

"So that's why his sentence was so lenient." Ryan had wondered. But then, his biological father had received only five years for a nonconsensual-rape conviction more than twenty years later.

"You knew about his record," Audrey said, as though only now realizing that.

"Yeah."

"And you didn't tell me."

"It wasn't my story to tell."

"Most people would have done so, anyway."

"I'm not most people."

"You didn't want to prejudice me against him."

With his beer held between both hands in front of him, Ryan stared at the floor. "The conviction was almost forty years ago, the sentence indicative of mitigating factors, and he's been clean as a whistle ever since. I knew you weren't in danger." There was more he owed her. Or maybe he owed her nothing.

Maybe he was meant to struggle alone with finding a way to accept Mark Dalton. To forgive him.

Maybe Ryan was alone in his belief that some things were meant to be sacred, and no matter if a man had been drugged or not, there should be something inside him that stopped him from participating in a three-men-to-one-girl foursome.

"Do you think Leonard was wrong to have sex with his girlfriend?"

Ryan had no idea why he was pushing this. He lived within rigid boundaries, but that was because they were right for him. They spoke truth to him. He didn't expect others to live by his conscience. Did he?

"I think it was understandable," she said, not helping him out at all. Would she understand Mark's situation, too?

"They'd been going together for a couple of years,"

Audrey continued, defending a man who'd been irresponsible with his penis, leaving Ryan feeling more foreign than ever. "They had normal, healthy needs."

"So you don't think he should have been punished."

"I do. But I think she should have been, too. From what I heard, she wanted to make love as badly as he did. Maybe more so. He was leaving for college and she wanted to have something to hold him to her. She was afraid of losing him to some college coed."

Ryan was surprised to hear her, a woman, blame the girl.

"But he was older. The man. It was up to him to stop things." The view was old-fashioned. But still true.

Frowning, Audrey cocked her head as she looked at him. "Why?"

"Because." *Real mature, Mercedes.* "A penis is a wonderful thing, but responsibility goes side by side with the incredible pleasure it provides. Women definitely affect its responses. They can cause it to get hard. But that doesn't give a man the right to stick it where it doesn't belong."

"Even if she gives him the right?"

"If you tell me I can use your state ID to get into the courthouse without security screening, and I do so, am I blameless?"

"Of course not."

"If I got caught, I'd be charged and convicted and sentenced."

"Yeah."

Her eyes glistened as she stared at him, as though assessing if he was for real.

"Yeah," he repeated.

Some things were still black and white.

CHAPTER FIFTEEN

NESTLED IN RYAN'S ARMS on the wicker couch in her sunroom Saturday evening, Audrey sighed. She belonged here. She didn't. The war inside her raged, battle after battle, with no clear victor.

"What was that for?" His fingers were rubbing up and down her arm. She didn't want him to stop touching her. Ever.

"I'm confused."

"Okay, let's talk about it."

Listening to the deep tenor of his voice, to the words he said, she could close her eyes and believe that Ryan Mercedes was a member of her own generation.

"I feel so safe here."

"In your house? That's natural," he said softly. "This is your home. You've been here a long time."

She almost left it at that. Except that she wasn't going to be a coward anymore. Today, finally facing the truth about herself, finally having the courage to face her life, had netted her a family.

And fear of the unknown had robbed her of that very same family for many years that she would never get back.

"I meant here." She tapped his chest. "Against you. In your arms."

His silence allowed the sea of doubt to wash back up to the shores of her mind. And heart.

He was only twenty-two. Far too young to take on the responsibility of a thirty-five-year-old woman's emotional baggage.

"Does that scare you?" she asked.

"Hell, no!" Ryan moved only enough to meet her gaze, his hold on her body changing, but not loosening at all. Then, still holding her gaze, he added, "And yes."

Trying to pull away, Audrey fought back more tears. For a woman who rarely cried, she was doing far too much of it these days.

"Hold it," he said, holding her head to his chest with a gentle hand. "Let me explain."

Audrey lay still. She could have escaped if she'd wanted to. They both knew that.

"I love you so much it hurts," he started to say, his voice clear, though not quite steady. There was no mistaking his sincerity. "I want nothing more than to have you need me as much as I need you. And yet, is it fair to ask that of you? I'm rigid, I get that. I see what I see. I'm not sure I'm good for anyone on a fully committed basis. I expect too much. And then there's the other side of it. The obstacles our age difference presents. I know I can handle them, but what if you can't? The thought of having you, then losing you scares the hell out of me. Does that make sense?"

It did. So much. Too much.

"I can't make any promises, Ryan." But, God, how she wanted to.

"I'm beginning to realize that."

"Meeting my aunt and uncle today, hearing their story,

seeing what fear did to my mother all tell me that I have to listen to my heart, just like you're always preaching."

His arms tightened. "Well, then…"

"But I'm just as certain that we're meant to learn by our life's experiences."

"I agree with that."

"I saw my mother in myself today, Ry. I see her in me when I look back on some of the choices I've made. I'm too much like her. But instead of trying to hold on to love with manipulation and control, I do it by compromising myself."

"That's something we can change, sweetie. Something we can work on together. You just have to see that you'll be loved whether you do what I want or not."

"But don't you see, Ryan?" She sat up, looked at him. "I'm already doing it. Simply by being with you right now."

When he didn't say anything, she knew she was finally getting through to him.

"Maybe you want me because you can't have me. It's human nature."

"That's not my nature. But as you say, neither is this my nature." He sighed and she'd never seen him look so defeated. "I don't know what to say anymore," he continued. "I love you. I don't want to leave here. But I can't fight against both of us and the age thing, too."

Cold, hard tendrils of fear spiraled through her.

"You're leaving?" He had to eventually. She knew that. But…

"Of course not," Ryan said. His voice had lost its luster. "I just don't see a future for us right now. Can we let it all go for tonight? Just be together and to hell with the future?"

It was the dumbest suggestion he'd ever made.

"Yes," she said, forgetting to act her age.

AN HOUR LATER, in Audrey's bed for the first time, Ryan roused himself to ask, "Have you talked to your mother about Leonard yet?"

He felt Audrey shake her head against his shoulder, the movement brushing the sheets against his skin. Her sheets were a lot softer than his.

Thread count, she'd told him. He was off to the store again in the near future.

Right after he got out of her queen-size bed in the light-gold room filled with rose everything. Which wouldn't be that evening, if he had his way.

"I'm not sure what to say to her," she answered at last, her voice groggy, whether from sleepiness or spent passion, he wasn't sure. It turned him on, though. For now that was all he wanted to think about.

And who was he kidding? Audrey washing dishes turned him on. Or driving a car. Sitting on the corner of his desk at work. Talking to a client on the phone.

Answering her door.

Standing outside his...

"I wanted to talk to you first, see what you thought."

The words had him fully alert, all thoughts of sex fleeing. Couples ran life's decisions by each other. Real couples.

The thought thrilled him—and urged him to run as fast and as far as he could.

And yet his legs wouldn't move. Wouldn't disentangle themselves from the limbs wrapped around him.

This was time out of time, he reminded himself. An hour, or a day, just to exist.

So where was the harm in acting like a real couple? What was wrong with trying on the concept for size? his inner voice asked. How would they ever know if there was any real compatibility if they didn't explore a little bit?

And that reminded him...

"My mother sends her apologies." Seemed like a year ago since he'd told his parent he'd pass on her message. A year since he'd introduced Audrey to Harriet and Glen. "She feels awful for making you uncomfortable and would like you to come back. She promises to welcome you."

Her hand on his chest clenched, but she didn't move her head from his shoulder.

"She was being a good mother. Looking out for your best interests."

Ryan studied the art on the opposite wall—a series of children engaged in different activities and wearing different attire, from formal dress to swimsuits. "She was overstepping and she knows it."

"She loves you."

"And she's wrong about this one." One young boy on the opposite wall held up sparkling clean hands while the smile stretching his face from ear to ear was covered with smudges of what looked like chocolate. "Whether we make it or not, it won't be because of our age difference."

"Her concerns were valid."

"She didn't factor in the positives...the fact that I am in love with you."

"You don't know that."

"Yeah. I do."

"For now."

"Forever."

His focus was solely on Audrey as she twisted to meet his gaze. He wished he could read her mind. "I love you, too, Ry, and it scares me to death."

Knowing it was impossible, Ryan set about kissing away her fears. They were going to be there in the cold light of day. But he continued to apply his antidote regardless. He just plain didn't know what else to do.

AUDREY WATCHED the clock. Time was ticking. The evening was ending, turning into night. And then day would follow. She should rest. Sleep in Ryan's arms while she could.

She didn't want to miss a second of the time left with him.

"So your dad was a designer."

Apparently he wasn't ready to sleep, either. "Yeah." The idea seemed so foreign. "I don't think I've really digested the fact that Jeff was my dad. Leonard seemed like my dad to me." Turning her head on the pillow she was sharing with Ryan—the pillow she'd been sleeping on alone since she'd bought it a couple of years before—she looked for his reaction.

"Did you see pictures of him?"

"A whole album of them." She'd felt no kinship, but then, she'd been working under the assumption that her father had been alive all these years. Identifying with a man who, in his oldest pictures was still younger than she was now, seemed too far a stretch. "He was smiling in almost every one of them," she told Ryan, remembering the impressions she *had* had. "Aunt Becky says that he was a charmer—that he had a way of always making people feel good. She also said he had an uncanny ability to take things in stride."

"Like his parents' unexpected deaths and having a seventeen-year-old sister to raise?"

"And finding himself head over heels in love with another man's wife."

"You sound like you don't approve."

"I like Leonard. He deserved better than that."

"But you said he admitted of his own accord that things between him and your mother weren't good. And it sounds as though he found the woman he was really meant to share his life with. Through Jeff, as a matter of fact."

She hadn't thought of it like that. "I just don't feel...I don't know...any kind of attachment to him, you know? I finally see pictures of the father I've been curious about my whole life and I feel nothing at all. I could have been looking at pictures of anyone."

"You spent your whole life angry with someone for deserting you—and wondering what was wrong with you that made him desert you—only to find that you weren't deserted at all."

His lips were a little swollen. And it was no wonder, considering how many hours they'd been in her bed. Still, she was ready to make love again, always. The appetite she had for this man apparently couldn't be assuaged.

Was something wrong with her? Something that led her, a mature woman, to the bed of a young man? Or was this really that great emotion she'd been seeking her entire life but never found. Was it that once in a lifetime true love?

"I spent my whole life wanting to give him a piece of my mind." Wanting to meet the man who, with her mother, had created her. The man whose genes had made her who she was. "I'd like to have met him at least."

"I'm sorry, sweetie." Ryan moved in, kissing her softly on the mouth. "I'd hoped, when I nosed my way into this, that you'd find your father, be able to meet him, make peace with his desertion. Instead, you find that you'll never be able to meet him."

"True." And there was some disappointment in that. Probably a lot once the residual shock wore off. But… "At the same time, I found out that I wasn't deserted at all."

"YOU SAID ONCE that your mother blackmailed you the whole time you were growing up." They were in Audrey's kitchen, preparing a snack to take back upstairs.

"She did blackmail me," his gorgeous companion said. "Emotionally, at least." Dressed in a short white terry robe that barely covered her butt, Audrey had never looked cuter to him.

Or more vulnerable.

Adjusting the towel he'd hooked around his waist, Ryan bent to grab some vegetables from the fridge. "But from what your aunt and uncle said, it sounds as though she loved you. A lot."

"As much as she can love anyone."

Glancing over his shoulder, he noticed the lack of expression on Audrey's makeup-free face. There appeared to be no bitterness attached to the words. Just acceptance.

"You honestly don't think she's capable of loving deeply?"

"I don't know," she said, putting some dip into a little glass dish. He'd have stuck the container on the tray. "Maybe she could if she could get rid of whatever fear drives her. Maybe not. I figured out a long time ago that my mom needs me. I provide her with emotional security, and I guess that's a kind of love."

"That's you loving her. How does she love you back?"

"She cares about me," Audrey said, leaning back against the counter with her arms crossed. "But with her it seems more like the way people care about the walls that keep them warm, or the car that drives them safely or the money that provides life's necessities."

"She cares about you for what you do for her, not for what she can do for you."

"I guess."

"Does she ever do things for you?"

"Sure she does. She's always wanting to know what I'm dealing with, wanting to offer advice…"

"The well-meaning, painful kind?"

"Not always. My mom's a smart woman. In a lot of ways she's very savvy. She deals with people every single day and often has good insights."

Not at all the picture Ryan had painted in his mind.

"It's just that she has this tendency to follow up on whatever advice she gives to make sure you took it."

Ah. "She wants to control you."

"Yeah, but it's more than that. It's like a personal victory to her every time she gives advice that I follow and she turns out to be right. Like she somehow becomes more valuable to me. I swear, she has advice-accepted-and-I-was-right notches on her bedpost. Counting them every night is what gives her the security to go to sleep."

Ryan might not have been an adult for fifteen years, but he'd been around enough to know that nothing in life was simple.

In her mother's world, everything had conditions. Everything.

"It's more about being right than being loved."

"Exactly. She's right in the name of love."

"Because to her, love is a tally."

"Yes."

"Sounds like a pretty painful way of life she's chosen,"

he said. "She's negating the ability and right to be loved just because you exist."

Audrey's hand on his back sent chills of awareness throughout his body. Awareness of her. Of loving her.

"You have this uncanny ability to put into words things that are usually too nebulous to fully understand."

"I cut to the chase, you mean."

"Maybe." Coming around, she leaned against the counter next to him, facing him, her hip touching his. With her fingers she softly explored the side of his face. He could easily stand here forever.

"I tend to think that you have the gift of real insight," she said, admiration shining from her eyes.

"More like I spend too much time in my head, analyzing everything to death." It was a fault he'd long ago recognized. "In any case, the bottom line here is that to your mother, love is conditional."

"With my mother, everything is conditional."

"So when we go see her tomorrow, you need to lead into telling her about having met your aunt and uncle by letting her know how valuable her opinions, her side of the story, is to you, too." Ryan talked fast, knowing how much was resting on the next few minutes. He was pushing. He knew that, too. He just didn't know another way. "She's going to be feeling insecure if she thinks that you don't need her anymore, or if you judge her and find her wanting. If you blame her…"

"Wait a minute."

"What?" Busted.

"What was that you said?" Her hands were planted on her hips as she watched him.

"About your mother's insecurities?"

"Ryan Glen Mercedes, don't play stupid with me. *We* are *not* going to meet my mother tomorrow."

"You said earlier that you had a lunch date with her tomorrow."

"I do."

"You said you wanted my opinion where she's concerned. I think I need to be there to give it."

"You going to go to my gynecologist with me, too?"

"If you needed me, I'd be there in a heartbeat."

"Ryan, stop this." Her voice cracked.

He turned, taking hold of her elbows as he bent to meet her at eye level.

"What's it going to hurt if I meet her?" he asked, instinctively using the tone he'd used with Takeisha Baker earlier that day. "Look at us tonight. We can't go to sleep, can't let each other out of our sight, can't lose a second of this time together. How's it going to hurt any less to see where this takes us and then break up, or break up now? Because I have to tell you, if I walk out of here tomorrow and we're done, there's nothing that's going to hurt more than that."

He was talking too much. And he couldn't seem to stop. Conviction drove him. Desperation drove him.

For the first time in his life he didn't have the answers.

"What are you suggesting?"

"That we give us a try that lasts longer than a moment. That way we know for sure."

"Are you forgetting all the things we talked about earlier? Your aversion to being part of a couple? My inability to maintain autonomy when I love? The agony my mother caused when she loved? Not to mention the fact that I am old enough to be your mother?"

"No." He had to be honest with her. "And I'm not sure we're going to make it," he told her. "But at the same time, I'm remembering about the wasted thirty-five years between you and Leonard and Becky. And I know how it feels right now, tonight, here with you. I ask myself, what do we listen to? Our heads or our hearts?"

"I don't feel good about us going forward."

"I know."

"But you want to go, anyway."

"I don't know what else to do."

"Walk away."

"*You* walk away."

"I am not taking you to meet my mother."

"So I'll drive."

"Ryan."

"Sweetie…"

She stared at him for so long he started to sweat. She was going to refuse to give them this outside chance.

"Fine." Ryan was so relieved to hear the word, he didn't mind the anger in the voice that delivered it. "But when this backfires and we're forced to see how impossible it is for us to even think about being together, you'll have only yourself to blame."

Fair enough. Blame wasn't what he was scared of.

RYAN MOVED, adjusting his legs—and the one of hers that was thrown over his waist. His breathing had quieted.

"You awake?" It was the middle of the night.

"Yeah." Ryan's arms tightened around her and Audrey

snuggled her face up to his chest. Nothing had ever felt so right.

She'd been lying awake for the past hour, her thoughts battling each other, worrying about lunch the next day, and life every day after that.

Audrey trailed a finger over the mostly hairless chest and around one of his nipples. Raw hunger for a man's body was new to her. Her passions had always been contained, soft nudges. Without real fire.

He shifted again, pushing her leg a little lower. It now rested across his groin—and a penis that was already half-engorged.

She moved her leg ever so slightly, back and forth, unable to ignore that vital part of him.

His hips lifted slightly.

And Audrey was filling up with desire for him. Her body ached, her belly trembled, and the liquid fire between her legs was back.

His penis, hard and hot, pressed against her inner thigh, again and again, establishing a rhythm that was already familiar to her.

She shifted again, moving over enough to find the tip of him with her wet opening, and slid down on him, accepting him as part of her, welcoming him home, while her head still rested against his shoulder, her torso plastered to his.

Her hips moved only slightly, back and forth across his groin, caressing him inside her warmth.

Ryan's hands were at her hips, holding them over him, as his body surged upward. Still without a word.

She held her hips firm, refusing to join him in the dance. Wanting to savor him inside her as though he'd always been there. And always would be. Filling her up with him. A part of her.

His hips dipped, as though he were going to pull out of her enough to surge back in. And she couldn't let him.

Audrey sat up, keeping his body still. "Are you sure this isn't all we're about? Some pheromone reaction we've fallen prey to?"

His hips stilled as his eyes narrowed on her in the darkness. "Is that what you think?"

Audrey froze, past and present mingling together in a confusing mass of emotion-induced panic. "I don't know what to think."

Sliding backward, she intended to release Ryan's body from hers, but he was there, his hands on her backside, holding her to him.

"What just changed?" he asked, his voice soft.

"Nothing."

"Don't lie to me, Audrey."

"I'm not…" Her hands on his chest, she stared at him in the shadows cast by the nightlight she always left glowing. "Yes, I am."

"Thank you."

"For what."

"Being honest."

He wasn't moving at all. And suddenly, sitting on him, accepting his intimacy, was far more than she could bear. And she knew that their little idyllic fantasy had ended.

The past had caught up with her. Landed.

CHAPTER SIXTEEN

"WHEN I WAS SIXTEEN I had a crush on my band instructor," Audrey said, sitting next to Ryan, in the robe she'd pulled on, her arms wrapped around her legs as she spoke of something that had been locked up and buried for nineteen years. And, she'd thought, forever.

That feeling of doing something dirty with her body. Using her body to feel loved.

"You played in a band?" He'd pulled the covers up past his hips. His gaze was intensely focused on her.

He knew there was something more. And, she suspected, was taking time to prepare himself. She considered dropping the key to her past right back into the dark abyss she'd created for it all those years ago.

"Until I was sixteen."

He didn't move, other than to cross his arms over his chest. "What instrument did you play?"

"Flute."

"I can picture that. Do you still have it?"

"No."

"What did he look like?"

"Medium height. Dark hair, a little longer than what was completely respectable."

"That's what you liked? His long hair?"

"No." Going back was far more difficult than she'd anticipated—and she'd known it wasn't going to be easy. "He had this way of looking at you that made you feel as though you were the only person alive. He was a musician. Intense. Kind of earthy and rugged and…"

Stopping, Audrey started to sweat. She'd been such a twit. Paid such a huge price.

And no matter how many years passed, she couldn't change the past. Couldn't make it go away.

She turned her head toward him, and he said, "So what happened?" His eyes had narrowed.

"You don't want to know."

"Probably not, but I have a feeling I need to know."

She opened her mouth, but couldn't find the words to express what she felt—either then or now. Couldn't find a way to tell this young man what a fool she'd been.

"Tell me."

"Can't you guess?"

"Probably," he said again. "But I think it's important that you tell me."

"The summer before my junior year, we were at band camp."

"And?"

"One night after the campfire, he came on to me."

"Came on to you, how?"

"He'd asked me to help him carry some stuff up to the main house. Said he'd walk me back to the cabin I was sharing with five other girls."

She paused, waiting for Ryan to let her off the hook. He simply continued to hold her gaze with eyes that were encouraging, loving and relentless at the same time.

"I was shivering on the way back and he put his arm around me to warm me up."

"How old was this guy?"

"Twenty-four."

Older than Ryan was now. The irony wasn't lost on her.

"He told me I was different from all the other girls. More mature. He said he'd never met anyone like me."

Ryan didn't move. Not a muscle. Anywhere.

"This is too difficult."

"What doesn't kill you makes you stronger."

He had an answer for everything.

Audrey took a deep breath. "He said he'd been fighting his feelings for me all year."

"Go on."

"He said that when I turned eighteen, graduated, he wanted to marry me."

She couldn't tell that Ryan was breathing, he was so still. Silent.

"By the end of camp, I'd slept with him. And by the end of the summer he'd introduced me to his twenty-three-year-old fiancée."

Even in the shadows she could see the tightening of his jaw. But Ryan said nothing. For a very long minute.

"Was he prosecuted?"

"No."

"Why not?"

There were some things that just stay buried. Even in moments that were time out of time.

"I couldn't bear the idea of the scandal. My shame was hard enough to live with. The thought of others knowing what I'd done, how immoral I'd been, how stupid—"

"You were a victim."

"I was stupid."

"You were a young girl trusting a man who was in a position of authority over you. You were supposed to be able to trust him."

"I knew sleeping with him was against school rules."

"Did you also know it was statutory rape?"

"Not then, I didn't." Nor did she know that, when he'd denied the whole thing, saying she'd made it up because she'd had a crush on him, come on to him, and he'd gently told her no, there'd been a way for her to prove differently.

"Did your mother know?"

"Only that I'd slept with a boy and he'd dumped me."

And only because, in the end, she'd had to tell her.

"I'm only guessing here, but based on what you've said about her, it would stand to reason that she used that mistake as proof of your poor judgment with an end goal of convincing you to trust her judgment, instead of your own."

He was good. Far too good.

"Change *used to* to *still uses* and you're pretty much on the mark."

"And the bastard? Whatever happened to him?"

"I have no idea. I was…sick a good part of my senior year and only ran into him once in the hall. I pretended I didn't know him, and he acted like he didn't see me."

With his hand in her hair, lightly caressing her, Ryan kissed her forehead. "I'm so sorry, babe. So sorry you were hurt. That you had to go through it alone."

He had no idea. Nor was he going to.

"It's okay," she said, her heart braced, as always. "It was a long time ago. I learned a hard lesson, though. And if this is some kind of adult repeat, a pretense to get sex, then let's just get the sex and be done with it."

"Is that how you feel about it?"

She didn't know how she felt. Scared. Unsure. Stupid. And weak.

"I didn't feel that way about it back then." It was a cop-out. And also the truth.

"What are you telling me?" He had that intent look again.

This was her chance. The chance to tell him that this relationship wasn't going to work. She could still salvage part of her heart.

"I'm not telling you anything," she finally admitted.

"You're not getting ready to tell me you don't want to see me anymore?"

He'd never sounded more like a kid than he did in that moment. It should have been enough to push her forward. "No, Ryan, I'm not getting ready to tell you that."

"So then what does it matter what you call it? Sex, making love—the important thing is that we're going to continue together until we find out what it is."

Ryan sounded so calm. So confident. Audrey pretended to believe him.

CHAPTER SEVENTEEN

RYAN DIDN'T KNOW what he'd been expecting at lunch the next day, but the petite, well-dressed woman who stood at the table as they approached, then gave Audrey a hug and a kiss on the cheek, wasn't it.

"Mom, this is Ryan."

Amanda Lincoln's glance was shrewd as she looked him over, taking in the sandals he wore without socks, and probably every single hair on his legs as well, Ryan thought.

"This better be your detective, Audrey Lynn."

Glancing at Audrey, Ryan caught the embarrassment on her face before she could turn her face away from him.

"I hope I am, too, ma'am," he said, taking the seat opposite Audrey's mother. Audrey had her nose. And cheekbones. But there the resemblance ended. The older woman's eyes, while brown, had no depth. No sparkle.

"I told you to call him, and I was right, wasn't I?" Amanda said, leaning in to her daughter. "If you're bringing him to me, he must be important."

Audrey had told her mother about him? She couldn't have given him a nicer gift.

She looked over at him, putting a hand on his leg under the table. A trembling hand.

"Yes, he is," she said.

Ryan covered her hand with his.

"SO, RYAN, HOW LONG have you been a detective?"

Audrey's stomach clenched around the little bit of salad she'd nibbled at.

"A year."

"Oh." Amanda's eyebrows rose with the "I see" tone in her voice. Audrey knew disaster was about to strike.

They'd almost made it through lunch, too.

"You were a police officer for a long while before that?" her mother asked, dotting her mouth with her napkin in spite of the fact that not a single spec of anything would dare leave itself sitting on her person.

"A couple of years."

Amanda put down her napkin. "That's it? You made detective in record time, then. Did you have previous investigative experience?"

Ryan's look in Audrey's direction was a warning—and perhaps an apology—and she knew she should never have brought him to lunch.

"I have no formal, professional investigative experience, Ms. Lincoln," he said, using the same tone he'd used while charming her mother with answers to her many questions about his favorite television shows, what kind of wine he drank and what he thought of the current presidential delegates. Audrey had yet to tell her mother about meeting Leonard and Becky Wilson. "I have no former professional experience at all. I am, in fact, a somewhat recent high-school graduate. Class of 2004."

Amanda's jaw dropped. As did the glass of tea she was holding.

And while Audrey tried to stay out of her mother's direct line of fire, Ryan, the consummate gentleman, calmly helped clean her mother up.

"THAT COULD HAVE BEEN worse." They were two streets away from the restaurant before Ryan broke the silence in the car.

"Just wait, it will be," Audrey said, staring straight ahead. "My cell phone should be ringing any second now. Please take me home and let's get on with our lives. Alone."

Ryan wasn't prone to hot bursts of anger. His ire was usually of the slow-burning variety. Which was maybe why he didn't contain the shot of pique that rent through him.

"You're a fraud, Audrey Lincoln, you know that?" There was no teasing in his tone. No kindness. Only weeks' worth of frustration. And a fear that he was finding harder and harder to contain.

"What?"

He didn't blame her for looking so shocked. He'd only once come close to talking to her that way and he'd stopped, calmed, after one word.

He didn't much talk to anyone that way.

"Look at you. You say you can't stay away from me, but the truth is you're looking for excuses to get away."

He executed a turn, then another. Watching his speed, but only barely. He could get away with nine miles over. Four, once he got to Audrey's neighborhood.

"How do you figure?" Her expression, when he took a quick glance at her, was not encouraging. He couldn't tell if she was pissed, or retreating to that place she'd been hiding all her life. He only knew she wasn't open to him.

Fine. Apparently he was going to have to wise his twenty-two-year-old baby-ass up and be done with this whole thing. It took two to have a relationship, and even he could figure out that one plus zero didn't equal two.

"Yeah, I admit that our age difference is going to present some challenges along the way," he said, not trying to filter at all. "But they aren't our biggest problem. My rigidness isn't, either. *You* are."

"Okay, we've established that you can point fingers, Ryan. Now how about backing up that childish act with something substantial? Or don't you have anything? Things didn't work out like you'd planned, my mother didn't take your age in stride as you'd apparently hoped, and now you're throwing a tantrum—"

"Audrey," he interrupted.

"What?"

"Shut up."

"Another juvenile respon—"

"Talk about pointing fingers, this one's coming right back at you, my dear," he said, holding his temper in check with effort. What in the hell was the matter with him? He'd mastered self-control years ago.

Unless he was around this woman.

And that meant being with her took away his control, Ryan realized with a sickening in his gut. Shit.

"How is it coming back at me?"

"You're the one acting like a child, Audrey. All scared and hiding and trying to keep yourself safe. You just spent the past hour with some important news to share and, instead, sat back and listened to idle chitchat. Your mother still doesn't know you met your aunt and uncle. My God, you were even afraid to tell her how old I was. You were going to go all the way through lunch and leave without ever letting her know that, either."

"Just because I don't happen to think it's wise to make an announcement doesn't mean I'm a child."

"The mature way to handle a problem is head-on." As quickly as his anger had come, it disappeared. He couldn't be mad at Audrey. She wasn't perfect, but no one tried harder than she did.

Her silence was Ryan's first indication that she was ready to really listen to what he had to say.

"I am completely certain that when we believe something, we make it happen," he said quietly, and even then his voice sounded too loud. He turned up the air conditioner. Maybe a little cooling off would help both of them.

"I've heard that before." He couldn't tell if she believed it or not.

"Every time you say you know it's not going to work strikes a chord of fear in my heart," he said. "You're manifesting our failure."

Signaling their exit, Ryan changed lanes. Turned off the freeway. Past one neighborhood. And another.

"I'm scared." He almost missed her words.

"I know," he said, wishing he could hold her hand, even while he needed his distance. "Me, too."

"I do love you, Ryan." Her eyes were glistening as she looked at him.

"And I love you."

But he was beginning to realize that love wasn't going to be enough.

"WELL, BIG BOY," Audrey approached the man sitting in her living-room chair, with somewhat false determination. "What do you want to do with the rest of our Sunday afternoon?" He wasn't leaving. She wasn't telling him to go.

But she had no idea what to do with him.

"Besides celebrate the fact that we came through our first fight with minimal damage, you mean?"

He was so Ryan. Putting everything right there on the table in front of them. Making them face life in all its glories. Good and bad.

"Yeah, that's what I mean." She'd been more apt to go back to pretending that they were one moment in time with no outside—or inside—forces working against them.

"I usually stop by to see Marcus, but his parents took him to Cleveland to see his aunt and cousin this weekend."

"We could try to catch up on some of the sleep you've lost." What in the hell was the matter with her? She wasn't the type to use sex as a means of escape. Abhorred the idea, actually.

"Are you coming on to me, woman?" Ryan's expression was stern. The hand between her legs told a different story.

And she was going to let it. Regardless of the breakup she knew they both knew was coming, she wanted him. Needed him.

"Depends." She licked his lips.

"On what?" He nipped her tongue.

"On whether or not I'd be successful if I were." She tried to laugh and almost cried. They weren't meant to be but, God, she wished they were.

"Aha. Afraid to commit, even now, huh?" he asked, pinning her with a stare that she'd seen intimidate more than one person on the other end of his handcuffs. "You have to be sure you'll be okay before you try? Do you have any idea how much of life you miss by letting fear hold you back?"

God, yes, she knew. She'd lost an entire family. But this

wasn't about fear. It was about learning from life's lessons. It was about facing reality.

And, maybe for one more moment, it could be about forgetting all that.

Standing, Audrey stepped out of her sandals and reached for the hem of her dress. Pulling it up slowly, in spite of the fact that, in this broad daylight, he'd see every dimple on her thighs, every imperfection on her body, she showed her teacher what a good pupil she could be.

Ryan said he loved her. *Her.* Not some ideal of what he wanted her to be. So she'd give him her. All of her.

And show him that she'd never be enough.

RYAN'S ENTIRE BEING responded to the woman stripping before him. Her skin glistened in the sun's rays, making her more angelic than human.

If he'd ever doubted that joys existed beyond his ability to imagine, he no longer did. He wanted every inch of her.

Standing, he undid shorts that had grown uncomfortably tight, pulling them and the underwear beneath them down only enough to release the evidence of his reaction to Audrey's stunt. The dress came over her head and her eyes widened, focused completely on his groin, then raised to meet his gaze.

"You, uh, got a problem there?"

"I don't think so. Unless you expect me to get these pants back on anytime soon."

"You really should do something about that. There might be an...emergency...or...something." She was staring again.

Tempted to take a hold of himself, just to call her bluff, Ryan resisted. "I'm not sure how to do that," he said, instead.

"Can I help?"

He met her gaze again, feeling the pressure build inside him as she drew closer. If he didn't think of something else, like having to clean Delilah's litter box, he was going to humiliate himself all over her living-room floor. "I don't know," he said, embarrassed by the strangled note in his voice. "What do you think?"

"I think—" Her cell phone rang. Audrey stopped. Glanced toward the couch where she'd dropped her purse—then back.

"I think…" The phone continued to ring. She glanced over again.

Ryan waited. Remained standing there in all his glory.

And then she was before him, staring into his eyes with promises that were probably going to haunt him for the rest of his life.

"I think I can." There was fear mixed with the desire in her gaze.

And Ryan was done playing. Pulling her against him, he kissed the breath of his life into her. And prayed it would somehow be enough.

A COUPLE OF HOURS later, Ryan was completely dressed again, ready to go home and feed Delilah and let Audrey get some preparation done for the breakfast meeting she had the next morning. He stood at the door, watching as she hung up from her voicemail.

"What did she say?"

"There were six messages. One a confirmation of my

meeting in the morning, and four from kids who needed to talk." Suddenly she felt like shit. A selfish shit.

"You don't owe your life twenty-four/seven to the work, babe." His face froze as he stared at her, his words hanging between them.

"I can't believe I just heard Detective Ryan Mercedes say that."

"To be honest, I'm not sure where it came from, either," he said, his voice without vigor, and she knew it was only a matter of time.

Ryan was Ryan. By his very nature, he wasn't going to be able to accept the changes being with her brought to his life. And he was beginning to see that.

He reached for the door. And though every instinct in her body screamed at her to go to him, to give him a goodbye kiss that would bring him back to her, she didn't move.

He was leaving. She didn't know when she was going to see him again. He went back to work the next night, which meant they'd be living in different worlds again.

"What did your mother say?"

He'd moved away from the door. Was standing right in front of her.

"She said that while she finds it embarrassing that her thirty-five-year-old daughter has chosen to have a boy-toy, she would advise, if I really care for you, as opposed to engaging in a sexual fantasy, that I give this relationship every chance to succeed."

"Engaging in a sexual fantasy?"

She'd known people weren't going to understand.

"She's leaving on an extended buying trip but wants to have lunch with us when she gets back." She couldn't look at him. A month seemed like an eternity right then. What were the chances that she and Ryan would even be friends a month from now?

"She wants to have lunch with *us*."

"Yes." Audrey tried not to hope. Or to build anything substantial out of her mother's pseudo-approval. She was thirty-five. Didn't need her mother's acceptance. She wasn't going to do anything just because her mother wanted her to do it. Not again. Not ever again.

"Did she suggest a date?"

"A month from Wednesday."

With a finger under her chin, Ryan lifted her face. "Nothing like planning ahead. Does she expect an answer right now?" he asked.

They both knew they couldn't give one.

"This is my mother, Ryan. She doesn't ask, she gives edicts. I'm sure she assumes we'll be there."

"If we're together, we will be."

And that, pretty much, was that.

"I'm going," he said, turning to the door. "I'll be back in a couple of hours."

"You're coming back?" It didn't occur to her to be upset that he was telling, not asking. There was too much else to care about at the moment.

"I'd like to sleep with you tonight. Is that okay with you?"

His gaze demanded honesty. "Yes. But…"

"Don't worry, Audrey, I'm not putting the condo up for sale. Or bringing Delilah with me."

"I like Delilah."

"Yeah, well, she's not really fond of traveling and I never

had her declawed. It's best for my skin if she stays right where she is." Turning, he reached for the door handle.

"What's going on here, Ryan?" she blurted to his back. She couldn't let him walk out on her with a promise to be back—but only for a night. "We keep playing with these moments out of time. When do they become back in time?"

He didn't turn around. "I think maybe right now."

"What does that mean?"

Silently he stood there. Let go of the door handle. And slowly turned. "I expect you're going to think this is crazy and come up with all kinds of reasons why it's a bad idea, but I think we should try living together for a couple of weeks."

She started to speak but Ryan held up a hand. "I know, I'm hearing all of the reasons why it's a bad idea from my own inner critics. But I just don't see any other way," he continued. "Think about it, Audrey. We're having sex. We say we care about each other. We keep finding ourselves together, yet we both know that it's not going to work. So why drag it out with months of weekends in bed and stolen meals through the week while we both dread the inevitable? Let's just face this thing. Let it take its course and end up on the other side, whatever that turns out to be, wiser people."

She wanted to argue. Knew she should argue. She opened her mouth to argue. They could as easily face it by ending their relationship right now. But she couldn't find the words to say so. Neither one of them was ready to end it. He was right, of course, that the agony would only be prolonged if they were weekend lovers.

"As soon as I make one choice that I know is not right,

just to please you, you're out of here," she said. "As soon as I start to feel like I have to beg for your love, you leave."

"Fine."

"And as soon as you start to feel cramped, you go."

"Agreed."

"Okay, then."

"Okay."

Without another word Ryan turned back to the door, pulled it open and left.

He was going to be moving in with her.

And she'd never felt more distant from him.

CHAPTER EIGHTEEN

THERE WERE PROBLEMS WITH living together. Other than the obvious difficulty of having to leave for work while his lover was snuggled under the covers going to sleep.

Ryan had no time to live his private life privately.

"Hi, Ry, it's just us. We haven't heard from you in several weeks and wanted to make sure you're okay. Give us a call. I love you."

Ryan listened to the end of his birth mother's message on his way home from work almost a month after he'd taken Audrey to meet his parents. Listened and felt guilty as hell. Sara was still so vulnerable where he was concerned—still that young girl who'd been forced to give up the baby she both loved and feared. The son.

And a grown woman, a mother in spite of the years she hadn't mothered.

He should have called her.

Just as he should have gone back to see his adoptive parents.

Instead, for the past weeks, he'd been living in no man's land with the woman he still couldn't get enough of. And Delilah.

He'd brought the cat over after the first couple of days of running home to feed her. The damn creature had her nose out of joint for the first couple of weeks, refusing to come out from under the living-room couch except to eat—and then only when the house was vacant. Or Ryan was asleep.

Turning onto Audrey's street, his gaze went immediately to the bedroom window, looking for the light that would signify that the love of his life was awake. Seeing it, he glanced farther down, to the tiny bathroom window. It was illuminated, as well.

She was in the shower.

If he hurried, he might be able to join her.

RYAN HAD DINNER cooking—spaghetti with sauce from a jar, frozen garlic bread and fresh broccoli—by the time Audrey's car pulled into the garage that night.

He'd made a decision and had to talk to her about it.

"Hey, babe," he greeted her, opening the door from the garage into the kitchen for her and taking her briefcase. They'd perfected the pretense of happily ever after in their day-to-day living—but only because they'd isolated themselves from the real world.

Instead of ending their time out of time and moving back into real time as they'd intended, they'd managed to stretch a moment into a month.

"Hi." She didn't quite smile as she leaned over for his kiss. He figured that she knew as well as he did that they were living on borrowed time.

"You're awfully quiet this evening," she said as they finished a mostly silent dinner.

Resisting the urge to jump up and tend to the dishes, which, in his other life, he'd have been more apt to leave for a day or two, Ryan remained in his seat. Tried to find the right words. Delilah jumped up onto the table and, willing to take the distraction, he shooed her away, giving her long, sleek back a stroke just because it was there.

Audrey was still waiting.

"We need to talk." He finally got the words out.

"Okay." Her lips tight, Audrey looked as though she was bracing herself. "Are you missing your place? Your independence?"

"It's not that." But in all fairness, he had to ask. "Are you?"

Her smile was more poignant than happy. "No, Ryan, you've been the perfect housemate."

Yeah, and perfection was an illusion. At some point one of them was going to have to quit trying so hard to make this work and just relax and be real.

They'd had a call from her mother, confirming their lunch on Wednesday. Audrey was planning to tell Amanda about Leonard and Becky then.

She'd seen the older couple several times over the past weeks, always while Ryan was home sleeping—deliberately, he was sure, but, true to current form, he hadn't called her on it.

He hadn't wanted to start a fight that would be the beginning of the end.

But he couldn't go on like this. He took her hand.

"I think it's time for you to meet Sara."

"Your biological mother."

"Yeah."

"Does she know about me?"

"Not yet. I haven't called her since I moved in here."

"I thought you were in touch every week."

"I was."

The reason for his neglect obvious, and now in the open, Ryan added, "But she's going to know about you within the hour. I need to stop and see them tonight. It's been too long. Marcus Ryan will probably be sitting up by now. Or talking or something. Anyway, I think you should come with me."

Audrey pulled her hand away, started stacking their plates and silverware.

"You go ahead this time, Ryan. Tell her about me and then we'll see." She stood and walked into the kitchen to put the dishes in the sink.

Ryan followed her, wrapping his arms around her from behind. "Please. We have to start facing things. And Sara's easy. She won't judge."

"Mm-hmm."

"I mean it."

She stood there, not turning on the water. "Just like you meant it with your mother?"

"That was different. Mom had a momentary blip in her emotional radar. She relapsed back about fifteen years in her role in my life and she apologized. Sara wasn't even known to me fifteen years ago, nor is our relationship such that she'd judge what I do or try to give me advice. We just have this need to spend time together on a somewhat regular basis."

Turning, Audrey studied him. "Then why do you have to push yourself to introduce me to her?"

She'd put him on one of the spots he'd been avoiding.

With his own hands firmly at his back, Ryan withstood her scrutiny. And opened his mouth.

"It's not just her. You meet her, you meet her husband."

And that was a bit too close to Ryan for comfort. Opening himself up that far wasn't wise.

But then, neither was this fragile, inauthentic existence.

"Mark? I thought you hardly knew him."

As always, Ryan's heart shuttered as he considered the man who'd fathered him. "I know him enough."

"So what's the problem?"

"Mark is." There, he'd admitted it. And was still standing.

"He's not going to approve of me?"

"I don't approve of *him.*" Ryan almost bit out the words. "They will both welcome you with open arms. They'd welcome an alien if I brought one to their house. It's not them meeting you I worry about. It's you meeting him."

Stepping away, Audrey rested her hands on the counter.

"Why? Because he's my age? Is that what this is about? You're afraid I'm going to relate to your parents more than I do to you? But wait, you said Mark is all that worries you, right, not Sara? So is this guy some kind of womanizer? A charmer that no one can resist? Don't you trust me any better than that?" She stopped the tirade only long enough to shake her head. "I can't believe this!"

To Ryan, her outburst was merely confirmation of what he'd already known. Their avoidance of anything that was a problem between them was building inner tensions that were escalating to explosive proportions.

"Audrey." Ryan took her elbows, held on. "Stop." He waited for her to look at him. "You're completely misunderstanding."

With doubt-clouded eyes, she waited. And Ryan knew his time was up. One way or the other. Either he gave more of himself to her. Or he had to leave.

He took a deep breath. Pictured himself walking out her

front door to the safety and freedom that awaited him at the condo he'd slept in that afternoon.

"I don't want you to meet Mark because I don't want you to associate me with him." Pouring out the depths of his heart was not what he'd intended. "I don't want to be colored by his genes in my blood. Period."

Her brow furrowed as she continued to stare up at him. "Why? You said once that he spent time in prison. Is that it? I meet up with a lot of ex-cons in my line of work. I care about their spouses and kids." Her soft voice almost broke his heart in that moment. Or the truth he had to tell did. "I certainly don't ever see those spouses and kids as a reflection of their husbands and fathers."

"Mark is a rapist." In the end, there was no other way to say it. "I am the result of a gang rape when my mother was sixteen years old."

Audrey had to sit down. "I...don't know what to say." Or what to think. How to help him. How did you assist with understanding when you didn't understand yourself? She, whose everyday life was filled with troubled kids, had never come up against something like this.

"Your biological mother married her rapist?"

Ryan nodded.

"Tell me about it."

Seemed like the only place to start.

"They were at a frat party at a lake in Maricopa, a small community outside Dayton. Sara, posing as a twenty-one-year-old, was there as a rebellion against her far-too-strict sheriff father. Everyone was drinking. No one remembers much after that. Sara woke up the next morning with her father's coat wrapped around her naked body as he carried her away from the lake. Her clothes were strewn around on the ground where he'd found her, passed out."

Ryan paced around the table.

"A medical exam showed that Sara had been pretty brutally penetrated."

He made it around the table one more time. Audrey wanted to grab his hand as he passed.

"Later that afternoon a kid came forward, said he knew who'd done it. He named three freshmen. Later tests proved that all three of them had been with her that night."

"Oh, my God." She'd been hoping, in spite of Ryan's agitation, to hear that it had all been a mistake. That Sara and Mark had been secretly in love.

Or at least that the sex had been consensual.

As though just realizing she was there, Ryan gave her a hard look. And then sat. His elbows on his knees, he stared at his hands.

"All three were convicted and sent to prison. Only Mark is still alive."

Alive and married to his victim? How in the hell had that happened?

"But not necessarily your father."

Ryan glanced up at her, his lips twisting. "Oh, yes. He's my biological father. I submitted to DNA testing last year."

"You sound as though you wish you hadn't." She knew how to do this, how to help young people through times of emotional familial crisis. How to determine what they needed and how best to get it for them.

She didn't know how to sit in her home where she'd made love with a young person and do her job at the same time. Or how to ignore the fact that Ryan's struggles went a lot deeper than she'd thought.

"I don't know that it matters," Ryan said now. "Fact is, whether it was Mark or one of the other two bastards, I'm still what I am. The son of a rapist." His eyes were shadowed when he looked up at her. "How does anyone know what compels a man—or allows a man—to take a natural, God-given instinct and twist it into something devilish and sinful? Who knows if it's a temperament characteristic, the result of his environment or some kind of genetic mal-function that can be passed down?"

"Surely you don't think that." But ideas were occurring to her. Was Ryan so rigid, not out of an inordinately strong sense of right and wrong, but out of fear? Of himself? Of the darker capabilities possibly lurking inside of every human being?

Was his fear of his parentage why he'd been a virgin at twenty-two?

"I don't know what I think," Ryan finally answered, drawing out the sentence as though, if he withheld the words long enough, he'd be able to figure everything out.

"How long have you known that you were a product of the rape?"

"I found out for sure last summer, but I'd suspected since I was fourteen."

Suspected. And feared?

"You know the four general rapist profiles, Ryan. Most often, the act has nothing to do with sex, but with a need for power and or control. That need is bred in someone. Not born to them."

He nodded. Swallowed. Continued to watch her.

She wanted to take him into her arms. "What profile does Mark fit into?"

Running his fingers over his hair, Ryan sighed. "None." The admission seemed to come with difficulty.

"I investigated him last year," Ryan continued, his statement not surprising her. "The guy had a sizable savings and an A+ credit rating. He owned his classic-car-restoration business free and clear. His probation officer reported regularly that the state was wasting money by paying him to meet with Mark, but he enjoyed their visits tremendously. Mark's got a law degree. And I couldn't find a single person who had a beef with the guy."

"How long was he in prison?"

"Five years."

"And when he got out he never repeated the act or exhibited any other violent behavior?"

"No."

"But he was violent that night with Sara?"

"Not necessarily." He rubbed the back of his neck. "Someone was, and Mark was there, a part of it all. He had sex with her during the same incident involving two other men also coming inside her. But other than what can be told from the solid evidence, no one really knows what happened. No one remembered a thing the next day."

"That's odd in and of itself."

"We found out last year that their drinks had been laced with PCP." Ryan went on to tell her the rest of the fantastic story—the murder he'd suspected after years of teenaged research, the pushing he'd done, Sara's seeking out Mark and his agreement to help. The final discovery that Ryan was right—his grandfather had missed key evidence and the rape had been used as a cover-up to murder.

Audrey nodded. "It was a popular date-rape drug in the seventies, wasn't it?"

"Yeah."

"And none of them knew about it?"

"No."

"So if Mark was drugged, he wasn't really guilty at all."

"He had gang sex with a sixteen-year-old."

"PCP enhances sexual drive."

"But it doesn't obliterate all morality. Besides, Sara was a virgin. He should have been able to tell that. To stop himself."

"Unless he wasn't first."

"And then we're right back to the gang-sex part. He did it to her after other guys had already done so."

"Sara has obviously come to terms with Mark's part in the incident since she married him. And just had his baby."

"Sara's too steeped in guilt over her own part in the whole fiasco to point fingers. She wasn't supposed to be there at all. Had never had anything to drink before and went there purposely to get drunk. She pretended to be older than she was. Those guys had no way of knowing, even if they'd been sober, that they were engaging in statutory rape. And all three of them went to prison.

"Besides, she's the forgiving type. And she's too trusting."

Sara Dalton sounded like someone Audrey would have gravitated to if circumstances were different. Someone who might have been a friend—if not for the fact that Audrey was sleeping with the woman's twenty-two-year-old son.

Watching the expressions chase themselves across

Ryan's face—the disgust, distaste, fear—as his words rang in the quiet room, Audrey searched for a way to reach him.

"This is a gray area, Ry," she said softly. "There's nothing black and white about a man being drugged without his knowledge. Nothing black and white about actions resulting from hallucinogenic substances. How can he be held accountable for something he doesn't remember? Something he did because he was being controlled by an illegal foreign substance?"

"He couldn't help the PCP. But no one tied him up and stuck his penis inside a sixteen-year-old girl."

Ryan wasn't bending. Even a little bit.

Audrey tried another route. "How does he feel about what happened?"

"I don't know."

"You don't know?"

"I don't talk to Mark much."

"Do you talk to him at all?"

"Not really."

"Don't you think you should?"

"I don't know what to think. And when I don't know, I wait to act until I do know."

She couldn't argue that point.

IN THE END, Audrey went with Ryan to visit the Daltons. He was right—it was time for them to quit kidding themselves and face the fact that they had separate lives. They had to get back to living their lives.

They had to start seeing each other as they really were. Not as the fantasy they'd created.

As they were driving over, silent in his truck, Audrey

didn't miss the irony of realizing that her mother had been right again.

She'd been living in a sexual fantasy.

Glancing at Ryan in the fading light of day, she saw a different man than she'd seen before. His rigidity was suddenly not the completely positive trait she'd previously considered it. Standing up for what you believed was one thing.

Judging and condemning, something else entirely. Acceptance—forgiveness—was sometimes more important than right and wrong. If Ryan didn't bend a bit, life would eventually break him.

No one was perfect.

Sara Dalton, a strikingly beautiful woman with long, dark hair and warm, green eyes, stood with baby Marcus cradled against her chest an hour later. She'd asked Audrey to come see the nursery.

Remembering her time alone with Ryan's adoptive mother several weeks before, Audrey had been reluctant to be alone with the woman.

But with Sara, Marcus and Audrey out of the way, Ryan would be alone with his biological father. A man Audrey liked tremendously, a man she trusted even after only a couple of hours of acquaintance. Maybe some good would come out of the next minutes. For all of them.

Maybe Ryan's time with her, their time together, wouldn't be a total waste.

"I'm glad Ryan brought you over," Sara said. "I wanted to meet you." She'd said she had to change the baby before his nine-o'clock feeding, but she'd yet to put the baby down.

"I wanted to meet you, too," Audrey said, wondering if she dared enlist this woman's aid in helping Ryan to accept the past and the father who, while a strong, self-contained man, obviously needed Ryan's forgiveness. And approval.

Probably as much as Ryan needed to be able to give it.

"You did? Why?" Sara asked.

"Because you mean so much to Ryan."

Sara laughed self-consciously—the first time Audrey had seen a lack of confidence in the woman all night. "I'm not so sure about that. He's only known me a year."

"I'm sure. He gets a protective look on his face every time he mentions you. Your opinion matters to him."

Audrey felt so awkward standing there with a woman who was much more her peer than her son could ever be. The fear of losing Ryan grew stronger by the second.

"You think that's why he waited so long to bring you here?" Sara asked.

"I think that's part of it." Audrey was certain it was. Ryan didn't want to face the truth about them, about their age difference, about their issues, and Sara's existence pretty much put it right in their faces.

"I'm married to a man who raped me," Sara said softly, "which hardly leaves me in a position to judge others. Or to think that choices should be made based on what others think. Ryan is a smart man. A responsible adult more mature than many men twice his age. The fact that he's chosen to love you is not for me to question."

Narrowing her eyes, Audrey watched the other woman. The speech was too rehearsed-sounding to have come in the shock of the moment.

"You knew about me before Ryan called tonight," she guessed.

Sara didn't look away as she nodded. "Harriet called a couple of weeks ago."

After her conversation with Ryan. So much for Ryan's belief that the older woman would no longer meddle in his life—or his decision to love a woman thirteen years his senior.

"And?" Audrey asked. She was too old for game playing. Too weary of fighting the fears, the inevitability of her breakup with Ryan, to pretend.

"I don't agree with Harriet," Sara started to say, and Audrey was almost surprised, until the other woman continued, "But I am worried about Ryan."

"Because when I'm sixty and sporting cellulite and wrinkles he'll be forty-seven and catching the eyes of thirty-somethings?" And she'd be home begging him to still love her—feeling needy and alone, sixteen again, instead of sixty.

"No." Sara frowned. "Ryan's not that shallow. It goes deeper than that."

She needed to be home where her heart was safe. Where she could soak in a hot tub all alone, crawl under her covers and go to sleep.

"They say that boys go for women like their mothers," Sara said slowly, hugging her baby up to her shoulder, rocking him back and forth, as she looked Audrey straight in the eye.

"Right."

"Usually that refers to character traits."

Sara wasn't telling her anything new.

"Did you know that Ryan has been watching me, following my life, since he was fourteen?"

"Yes." But only because Harriet had told her.

"He said he needed to know me, to be close to me, but

that he couldn't hurt his mother's feelings by actually having me in his life."

That last part sounded like Ryan. And any number of other adopted kids.

"He's been investigating me since he first found out who I was."

"He had a natural need to know his mother," Audrey said, thinking of the lifelong hole in her existence where her father was concerned.

"Right. And while he could garner facts, he didn't know me, or my character traits, until this year. And now suddenly he's taken up with a woman who's practically my age…"

The blood drained from Audrey's face. She was cold in spite of the warmth in the nursery. The warmth outside.

The warmth in Sara Dalton's eyes. A woman who was more her peer than…

"You think he's with me because of my age. Because I remind him of you. You think he's trying to recapture some of the security he lost when you gave him away."

"I don't think it," Sara clarified. "I don't know it. I'm just afraid of it."

And just like that, Audrey was afraid of it, too.

CHAPTER NINETEEN

"THAT WASN'T SO BAD."

As she spoke, Ryan glanced over at Audrey, having difficulty reading her expression beneath the unnatural red glow from the stoplight above them. Something was different about her.

"What did Sara say to you back there?" He didn't have time to gently persuade Audrey to talk. He was due at the precinct in twenty minutes and was still five minutes from her house.

"Nothing, really. We chatted about the baby mostly."

"Yeah, I got that. And about the wallpaper and the fact that she still works for her father's foundation, but is able to do so from home..."

"So what did you and Mark talk about?" she asked, her voice conversationally sweet—and not personal enough. "It seems to have put you in a bad mood."

"Your prevarication is frustrating me," he countered. "Just tell me what she said and let's deal with it together."

"Ryan, I told you—"

"You aren't going to convince me that Sara had you alone and didn't mention you and me. Together." They were only two streets away from home.

"Actually, I mentioned us."

Now they were getting somewhere. He turned into their neighborhood.

"And?"

"She said, married to Mark, she's hardly in a place to judge and that she believes in everyone's right to make their own choices."

Not exactly an avowal of support, but it could have been worse.

"She also said that you're more mature than a lot of men twice your age."

He made a mental note to thank Sara. "So why are you being so distant?"

"I'm not. Really."

"You always say *really* when you're hiding something."

"And you're far too observant." She made a noise that sounded like an attempted chuckle, but it didn't work. "I'm just tired, Ry," she continued, reaching for her seat belt as he pulled into their drive. "And I'm worried about you. About you and Mark."

He had to go. Had work to do. Had to shut her up. And still, tonight, as with every night, he hated to leave her.

"My feelings for my biological father have nothing to do with us."

"What if someone drugged me, Ry? What if, not realizing that, I got in my car and drove and killed someone? Would you hate me, too?"

Rape was different.

And she had a point. He just wasn't ready to contemplate it.

"You're sure that's what's bothering you?" he asked,

instead, tending to what he had time for. "My aversion to my father?"

"Yes." There was conviction in the word. But she didn't look him straight in the eye.

He was going to be late.

"You have nothing to worry about there," he said far more quickly than he'd have liked. "No matter what you might do, I know you. And because of that, I believe in you. We'll talk more about this tomorrow, okay?"

"Okay." Audrey smiled, and there was no sparkle in her eyes.

"Everything's going to be fine. I promise."

She nodded.

But there was something vital missing from her goodnight kiss.

RYAN TOOK the long way home Tuesday morning, replaying, as he had many times during the night, last evening's events, not sure what to make of any of it. Not sure what to do.

Once again he'd managed to avoid the man whose body had fathered him.

"I'm going to check on Jerry," were the only words he'd spoken to the older man the night before.

Jerry, the fourteen-pound cockapoo rescue dog he'd given to Sara the previous summer when he'd thought she was going to be living alone, had been banned to the backyard when he'd jumped up on Audrey.

Ryan had stayed with Jerry until he'd seen the light in the nursery go out. He'd barely made it back to the living room ahead of the two women.

So he'd had an out the night before. He wasn't always

going to be that lucky. Which meant he was going to have to resolve his feelings for his father one way or another, he saw that now—even if that meant staying out of the man's home. He owed it to Audrey. To Sara and Marcus. And to himself. Sometimes life just plain sucked.

Audrey didn't mention anything about the night before when he joined her in the shower a few minutes later. Nor did she speak of the desperation he felt in her kiss during the extra fifteen minutes they took in the bed afterward. She didn't mention Mark or Sara or the tension lining their lives when she kissed him goodbye.

But he knew it was there. Knew, too, that it was time to get on with his life. No matter what that meant.

Thinking he'd go back to his condo to sleep, as he'd done once or twice during the past week, finding peace and solace in his aloneness there, Ryan picked up the phone first and dialed.

"Mark Dalton's office."

He didn't know what he'd expected, but a receptionist wasn't it.

"Is Mark in?" He couldn't bring himself to call the man Mr. as though he respected him. Or as though Mark deserved the respect.

"May I ask who's calling?"

No, you may not. Hand on his hip, Ryan almost hung up. Then he saw the wet towel Audrey had left on the end of the bed. A bed he needed to fall into and sleep life's problems away.

They were ganging up on him.

"Ryan Mercedes."

The click came almost immediately.

"Ryan? What can I do for you?" Mark sounded more hopeful than curious.

Ryan had hoped the woman had hung up on him.

"You doing anything for lunch?" He couldn't find the wherewithal to fake a nicety. Like hello.

"Nothing I can't reschedule."

"I need to grab a couple of hours of sleep. Can you meet me at Hathaway's at twelve-thirty?"

"Absolutely."

That was it. No questions asked.

Ryan really wanted to hate the man.

TAKEISHA BAKER mangled the tissue Audrey had given her.

"I need your help, Ms. Lincoln. I just can't do like they want. I get that my ma needs money. Especially now that Daniel's in jail. But I just can't do it. It isn't fair. It isn't right. Not to me or any kid."

"Terminating a pregnancy is a huge decision, sweetie." Audrey chose her words carefully. She'd been with the girl, from a doctor's appointment to a counselor and now here, for most of Tuesday morning. Her mother's boyfriend was in jail. Detective Dosendall was fully recovered. And it still wasn't over for the girl. "This is a decision that you will live with for the rest of your life."

"If I got a life." The girl's statement wasn't dramatic. Or threatening. It just was.

"If I have this baby, I've got no hope left, Ms. Lincoln. Even though it's Daniel's, I'd love it and be tied to it. And it wouldn't matter if I wasn't, my ma would take it and then it would always be there, waiting for me to love it. I'm only fifteen. I've got two years left in high school.

How long you think I'm gonna be able to keep going there if I've got a kid at home? I'll tell you what I'm going to have to do, Ms. Lincoln. Get a job, that's what."

Audrey listened with what she prayed to God was an unbiased ear. Her job was to try to give the young woman other options—which she'd already done—then to determine if Takeisha was mature enough to know what she was doing. To make certain that she had considered all of the ramifications of her choices.

Audrey's job was not to feel anything personal whatsoever.

"You've talked to the doctor," she said. "You know the risks. We've talked about your other options, about adoption and planned parenthood. About the halfway house."

It was a facility that Audrey had helped establish. One where she regularly gave free legal advice. One that she believed in with all her heart.

For the right girls. And women. In the right circumstances.

"Yes, ma'am," Takeisha said. "If I did this to me, if I was with a boy and made a baby, then I'd think I owed it to me and the baby and to God to see this thing through. But I didn't do this, Ms. Lincoln. I have a life, too. And I'm little and the doctor says I might have a tough time of it, being so young and all. I could end up like my ma, not being able to have kids someday. When I'm ready."

It was the girl's clear gaze that told Audrey they'd talked enough.

"Okay, sweetie. If you're sure this is what you want to do, you call me tomorrow and I'll advocate for you. And once the judge signs the papers, I'll go with you to have the procedure and to see that you get home okay afterward."

Fresh tears sprang to Takeisha's eyes. "Thank you,

Ms. Lincoln. I can't remember ever having someone be so nice to me…"

Audrey saw the girl out of the conference room in the city building that housed her little office, certain she'd made the right choice.

And then, back at her desk, with the door firmly closed, she sat down and cried.

"THE WHITE CHILI'S pretty good," Mark Dalton said, not even looking at his menu as he sat across the window booth from Ryan. As if on cue, their waitress, stopped by their table.

"You guys ready?"

White chicken chili was a Hathaway's special and one of his favorites. "I'll have a buffalo burger," Ryan said. "Coleslaw, instead of fries."

Buffalo had half the fat of beef, fewer calories, less cholesterol. And a nation of Indians who'd survived on buffalo meat had escaped even one case of cancer among them.

Ryan had just read so on the menu.

Slouched back comfortably in the booth, he busied himself with a slow stir of cream and sugar he didn't want in his coffee.

He'd dressed up for the occasion. Instead of his usual jacket and tie, he'd gone all out with an old faded T-shirt, cutoff shorts and flip-flops.

"I liked Audrey," Mark said after the waitress left. "You've made a good choice."

Ryan wanted to tell the man to wipe his lover's name from his lips and never say it again. "Thank you."

"How are things at work?"

Ryan looked at the other man—his biological father—

trying not to see the resemblances. "This isn't a social lunch," he said.

"I didn't think it was. You can barely be civil to me."

"So why make small talk?"

"Because I've learned that life is a lot more valuable when lived with kindness."

Valuable. A word Ryan might have chosen. He valued life. Which was why desecrating it was unforgivable. This man had ruined the life of a sixteen-year-old girl.

"I can't stand that you're my father."

"I know."

"I need resolution."

"Okay."

"I've never hated anyone before in my life. But I really think I hate you."

Mark didn't flinch. "I understand."

"What's with you?" Leaning forward, Ryan kept his voice low, but he couldn't hold back the venom. "You sit there so calmly taking personal insult as though you don't have a care in the world. Do you have any idea what you've done? How many lives you affected? Do you care about anything?"

Ashamed of himself, of his uncharacteristic lack of compassion, Ryan slumped back. Was it any surprise Mark Dalton brought out the worst in him? The man had given him dirty genes.

No, that wasn't right.

But what was?

Staring into his coffee, disliking the light-brown color because it signified weakness, he waited. Wondered how to extricate himself from the pointless meeting.

Mark wasn't going to say anything. Even now, he just sat and took. Did the man have no backbone at all?

The waitress brought their lunch, asked if they wanted anything else and didn't seem to notice that neither of them were talking. To her. Or to each other.

"Like you, Ryan Mercedes, I care about justice." Mark didn't touch the food in front of him. "I care about people. I care about right and wrong. I care deeply about my family. What I don't much care about is how others see me. I was branded a long time ago in a way that I will never be able to change. I had a choice back then. I could believe the branding, live it and become something I was not—a two-bit criminal who would spend his days on the dark side of life, driven by evil and revenge and a bitter spirit. Or I could live from the inside out, listening to my conscience, to my inner voice, and become the man I was meant to be."

Ryan's gaze had become locked on the other man. As though spellbound, he couldn't break away.

And he couldn't stand being there.

"You raped an innocent young girl." He pushed his burger away. The smell was nauseating him.

"You're a detective, Ryan. You, more than most, know that, in order to gain understanding, it's best to stick to the facts. The fact is, I had sex with a minor who I thought was older than I was. Whether that sex was consensual or not, no one knows."

Yeah, but…

"She was bruised where a woman should never be bruised."

"And I pray to God every single night that I was not responsible for a single one of those bruises. I am not that type of man. I cannot believe that of myself."

Eyes narrowed, Ryan said, "But the fact is, you don't know that you didn't do it."

"And that is a fact I will live with for the rest of my life."

And now Ryan had the man where he needed him, "Another fact for you—you participated in gang sex."

Mark's lips pursed—the only sign that Ryan had hit a mark. But the man never broke eye contact. "And that, Ryan, is the one fact I can neither escape nor live with. It will keep me from ever truly knowing real peace in this lifetime. I was celibate for twenty-one years because of it. But that's the funny thing about love. It's stronger than sin. Stronger than any mistake. It is the be-all and end-all. I know this. I believe this. And still, I have moments, days, when I feel unworthy of Sara's love. Of Marcus's love."

The sincerity in Mark's tone reached something inside Ryan. Touched him where he didn't want to be touched. Not by this man.

"But you feel worthy of my hatred." He was beginning to get a picture that scared the hell out of him.

"I understand your hatred," Mark qualified. "I've found in the past year of observing you while you're in my home, with my family, that you and I are a lot alike. In ways I wouldn't have thought were genetic. Were I you, I would hate me, too."

Ryan was not like this man. He just wasn't. He wouldn't allow such a thing. "So you just accept that."

"What choice do I have?" Mark sat back, still watching him. "I've done what I've done, Ryan. I can't change that. Nor can I change how you view what I've done. But along with that, I am who I am. Now there is something I *can* affect. Living true to the man inside me is where my power lies. Where my peace lies. And that is something I think you relate to completely."

Ryan rejected the comment. He couldn't share anything so intimate, so all consuming, with this…this…this…man.

"I don't expect you, of all people, to forgive me my past," Mark said. "Your very existence is marked by that night. That mistake. It works the other way, too. You are a constant reminder to me of a sin I will never escape. But I am alive for a reason, son. I have time on this earth to bring some small bit of good to this world. Time to learn how to forgive."

Ryan couldn't afford softness. His world was at stake. "Who've you got to forgive?" He sounded like a belligerent kid. But certainly Mark wasn't referring to Sara, a naive girl who'd lied about her age. Or a sheriff who'd been hell-bent on avenging his only child and missed a key piece of evidence. Neither of those things compared to what he'd done.

Mark's answer, when it came, touched Ryan again. "Myself." Mark stood, threw a twenty on the table. "You will never be as hard on me as I am on myself," he said. "So do what you have to do. Bring it on. I will stand beside you and take it for as long as I am alive. And if you ever need anything—*anything*—for any reason, you call me and I will be there. No questions asked."

Ryan sat there, staring after the tall, blond, muscular man, suspecting, for a wild second, that he'd just met his match.

Until he picked up the bill and, leaving all the food on the table untouched and the twenty as a tip, went to the cash register.

Mark Dalton knew all the right words. He wanted to suck

Ryan into the little family he'd created. Probably because he needed Ryan's approval for Sara's sake. And Marcus's.

He wanted Ryan to believe they were alike in ways that mattered most. He wanted Ryan to believe in his unconditional love.

Ryan wasn't convinced.

CHAPTER TWENTY

RYAN WASN'T in any better mood, or any less confused, when he got a call from the prosecutor that afternoon. Dennis Hall was working on the Takeisha Baker case. Defense for Daniel Wood was moving to suppress Takeisha's testimony in the hospital, as she was a minor who'd been questioned without parental supervision.

They were grasping at straws and Ryan was quick to assure Dennis that they'd taken all proper measures in securing the girl's testimony. He agreed to testify at the pretrial hearing scheduled later in the week.

And then Dennis passed on another piece of information.

"The poor kid's pregnant."

Ryan's heart sank. "She got a boyfriend that quickly?"

"The kid's Wood's."

"But they did all the medical procedures..."

"He'd been with her before."

Ryan swore. Sometimes life's timing was ironic. He'd spent a good majority of the day fretting over an ancient teenage pregnancy, and now this.

"It's what her mother wanted," Ryan said, more thinking aloud than anything. "The kid's in trouble. She has her whole life hanging in the balance, and she won't get any help from the one person whose job it is to be there for her."

"Don't fret that one," Dennis said. "She's got help. They assigned Audrey Lincoln to her case."

Audrey. Thank God. Some good news in an otherwise bad day.

"Rumor has it you and she are pretty good friends these days."

"Rumor is rumor because the truth is no one's business," Ryan countered easily.

"Got it. Well, for what it's worth, she could do worse."

"So could I."

Dennis's chuckle sounded tired. "Yeah, you could. That woman is a steamroller when it comes to looking out for those kids. She's already approached the judge, advocating on Takeisha's behalf for an abortion without parental approval or permission. It's on the docket for tomorrow morning…"

Ryan was sure Dennis finished his sentence. Said goodbye. But he couldn't testify to it. He hadn't heard a word past the roaring in his head.

And his heart.

THE HOUSE was dark. Hungry, having grown used to having dinner almost ready by the time she got home from work, Audrey couldn't help a stab of disappointment. That was quickly followed by fear.

Something had happened to Ryan. Otherwise, if he'd had to go out, wasn't going to be home for dinner, he'd have called.

Unless, she told herself as she pulled into the garage and saw his truck parked in the spot next to hers, he'd slept through his alarm. It would be the first time since he'd been there, but he'd told stories of having done it before.

And he'd been existing on little more than four hours or

so a day of rest for most of the past month. If he kept up that way for much longer, he was going to have serious sleep-deprivation issues.

Comforting herself with the knowledge that at least he hadn't left her yet, as she let herself quietly inside, she thought about the state of their freezer and canned-goods cupboards. They'd shopped together on Sunday—as they had every Sunday since Ryan had started staying with her. She could make chili. With onions and cheese. She'd fill a tray. With crackers and the sweet tea Ryan liked so much. And then she'd wake him with dinner in bed.

But first, she'd take a peek in at him. Just to make sure he was there. He slept naked most of the time, the covers curled around his hips, his long legs exposed, and Audrey felt a pang that took away her appetite as she faced the fact that she could be losing the right to the sight very soon.

Drawing close to the bedroom door, she walked on tiptoe. She didn't want to wake him. Which was why she'd turned on no lights in the windowless hallway. And prayed that she didn't trip over Delilah. The cat was underfoot a lot these days, now that she was growing more comfortable in Audrey's home. Not that Audrey was complaining. Having constant company was nice.

Better than nice.

When Ryan eventually left, she'd have to get a cat. Or maybe a dog. Or a bird.

In contrast to the hall, the bedroom was suffused with light. Which made it very easy to notice the empty, made-up bed, and beyond, the bathroom with towels hung and dry. There was no residual steam from a recent shower. If Ryan had gone to bed that day, he'd been up a while.

Backtracking through the house, her stomach in knots, Audrey thought back to that morning, to anything she might have said or Ryan might have said to explain this change in routine. The only thing out of the ordinary was that he hadn't called.

He called most every day when he got up.

She'd been so busy she hadn't thought much of the missed communication. Besides, there'd been a few days when he'd missed.

There was no sign of him in the den. No note on the hall table. Or the kitchen table. And in the living room...

There was Ryan. Sitting on the couch.

"Hi." She looked over every inch of him as she approached. And knew, when her searching reached his face, his eyes, that something was horribly wrong.

He was leaving. She'd known the time would come. In truth, she'd known it was coming soon. The life they'd been living wasn't natural, isolated as it was.

Because it was what they always did, every single time they came together, she leaned down for a kiss—as though the act could somehow fix all the problems between them.

He didn't move away. But didn't really return the kiss, either.

"Why didn't you say something when I came in?"

"I've been sitting here trying to make sense of the turns life has taken."

Her stomach recoiled as fear engulfed her. Panic. This was really it.

"What turns?" she asked when she thought she was braced to handle whatever came next.

Ryan shrugged, his eyes reflecting more emptiness than

hurt. She'd never before seen the old shorts and T-shirt that he was wearing. And wondered what the change signified.

Sitting down on the couch, a full foot between them, she thought about all that Ryan had taught her. About facing challenges. About not hiding.

"When are you going?"

"What?" He stared at her.

"I assume you've decided to move out." She pushed further. Getting through.

She could fall apart when he was gone. When he wouldn't see that she hadn't changed all that much, after all. Had grown hardly at all.

"Why would you assume that?"

Well... "Because it's obvious things aren't working out."

"We need to talk, Audrey." His voice didn't hold even a hint of the softness she'd grown used to. And begun to crave. "You're right, we can't go on like this."

"Okay." His bags weren't packed. She had a couple of hours, at least. "So talk."

"I had lunch with Mark today."

Apparently it hadn't gone well. "Tell me about it."

His eyes were still dark, dead, when he looked at her. "There's not much to tell. Just made me think about forgiveness. About right and wrong and what happens when the lines are so blurred there *are* no rights and wrongs."

"I'm not sure where this is going."

"Dennis Hall called today."

"What did he want?" And what did the prosecutor have to do with their private lives?

"He said that you're advocating for Takeisha Baker's abortion."

"That's right." Again, where was the connection between professional lives and their private one? Unless… She grew hot as realization dawned. Dennis must know about them.

He must have said something to Ryan that embarrassed him.

"It's clearly understood that no one in the courts, including judges, have to take on those issues. You can recuse yourself on the basis of personal morality."

"I know that."

Ryan nodded. Looked at her as though he didn't know her. "I would have bet my life that you'd take that out."

"Why? The child is fifteen years old. She was raped. This is her body we're talking about. Her life. I've talked with her extensively. Took her through all the necessary and recommended appointments. She knows what she's doing and I want to help her."

"Why? Abortion is killing an innocent child. Why would you want to be involved with that?"

"Ryan! You can't be serious. We're talking about a fetus that may or may not develop properly, in a body that is not ready for childbirth. Takeisha could die. What right is there in that?"

"My mother was raped, Audrey. If she'd had someone like you around back then, I wouldn't be here. I wouldn't even exist." His voice was almost hard and she knew that this wasn't really about abortion. The abortion was only the catalyst, the surface issue that was allowing him to play out what was really going on inside him. It was his excuse to get away from her and back to the self he was comfortable with. The self he knew and wanted to be.

He was right. They had a real problem. One Audrey knew was going to get much bigger as soon as she opened her mouth. She and Ryan might share some miraculous emotional connection, but they were clearly not meant for each other.

He was going to leave her. But not sometime in the future for another, younger woman. He was going to leave her because of the woman she was.

"I had an abortion, Ryan." Her darkest secret. One only her mother knew. And she told it in a monotone, as though it was no more momentous than a stock-market report. "That band director who denied ever having slept with me left me pregnant. My mother figured it out even before I did, and while I was still reeling from the bastard's betrayal, still coming to terms with the fact that I'd given myself to a man who couldn't have cared less, who'd used me, she had me at a clinic and was signing papers." Audrey didn't look back often, but the visions, the feelings, were as clear as though she was speaking of yesterday. "She told me that I had no choice, that I couldn't survive without her and she would absolutely not take care of me if I didn't do as she said. She reminded me that my father had abandoned me. And her. She threatened to take my car. My college fund. Mostly, she threatened to disown me—to take away the only love I'd ever known. And she said she was doing it all because she loved me so much. She was the adult, the one with experience. It was her job to look out for the two of us. She knew best. She pointed out instance after instance where she and I had differed and she'd been right…"

Audrey wasn't really talking to Ryan anymore. Wasn't even sure he could hear her. Or that it mattered.

At some point she fell silent. At some point Ryan looked at her. "Do you regret it?"

"Of course I do! How could I not?"

Turning, he seemed to come back to life. "Then do something about it, Audrey. Help this girl. Save her from a lifetime of the same regret before it's too late to take back..."

Hope died within Audrey as she listened to him. If only life were as black and white as Ryan saw it. Or as he pretended to see it.

As he needed to see it so that he had his out—his sure way to maintain permanent independence.

Maybe life really could be black and white. For someone like him.

But not for her. Most definitely not for her. Or the Mark Daltons of the world.

"I can't, Ryan."

"Of course you can."

"No." She shook her head. "I can't. For two reasons. One, while I greatly regret the abortion, I also know that I would have regretted having the child. I would either have had to kiss any kind of career and security goodbye, or I would have had to kiss my own baby goodbye. Ask Sara how that feels, how that affects the rest of your life, your beliefs in and about yourself."

"And the second reason?" He was looking at the blank television screen.

"I think, in Takeisha's case, this is the best decision."

"You mean that."

"I do."

He stood. "Then I guess there's nothing more for us to say. I'll go gather my stuff."

Jumping up, panicking in spite of the fact that she'd known this was coming, Audrey planted herself in front of him, her hands on his chest. "Just like that, Ry? You're going to walk out on me just like that?"

His eyes were sad, with no spark at all, for the minute he studied her. "We aren't the people I thought we were."

Tears choked her. "I'm not the person you thought I was, you mean."

"I…" Running his hand over his head, Ryan looked sick. Mentally and physically ill. Exhausted. "When you start compromising on right and wrong, where do you stop?" he asked. "You don't. You end up justifying and accepting until there are no standards at all and life is nothing but a free-for-all where the strongest and most powerful bully wins. I can't be a part of that, Audrey. There are some things I can't compromise on."

She held back her tears. Looked him straight in the eye. "I understand."

And she did. With a calm that was complete. She couldn't keep pretending, either. Couldn't keep watching every move, every word.

Not looking back at him, she stepped away, grabbed her keys and purse and left the house. Audrey drove for hours. Out to Alum Creek. Up toward Cleveland. On sideroads and byways. And by the time she returned home just after nine that night, her house was all hers again.

Ryan's key had been left on the kitchen table.

There was no note.

RYAN LAY IN BED Friday morning, tossing and turning. No matter how tired his body felt, no matter how exhausted his mind, his soul's struggle prevented rest. He'd done little more than work and doze since leaving Audrey's house earlier in the week.

Even after knowing her for only a matter of months, her

voice was in his head, one of his own inner beings, coaching him. Berating him. Reminding him. Critiquing him. Until he didn't know what was her and what was him. Was that his own inner critic? Or hers?

And in those rare moments when the two of them weren't ganging up on him, oddly enough, his biological father showed up. Mentally that was.

Mark hadn't preached. To the contrary, he'd left Ryan with the impression that Mark thought Ryan was on the right track. One of the few lucky ones. That his strong sense of right and wrong, his ability to live true to that sense, was a precious gift.

Except that he was alone. And Mark was not. Mark had it all. A wife he adored and who adored him. The real bone-deep kind of love that surpassed everything—including the darkest of pasts. He had a job he loved. A son. A baby son, that was. He had friends and a nephew who thought he walked on water. A sister who idolized him. A mother who had never stopped believing in him.

Punching his pillow—hard—Ryan turned over. Mark was a criminal. A rapist. Rapists were bad.

But Mark Dalton was not a bad man.

Ryan would have to be stupid and blind to think that he was. And while he'd done a pretty good rendition of being both over the past year, in truth, he was neither stupid nor blind.

And now was the time for truth.

Mark Dalton was a good man who'd made a bad choice.

And he'd paid for that choice—would continue to pay for it until the day he died. And beyond that was anyone's guess.

Certainly it was out of Ryan's field of knowing or responsibility.

Mark was what he was. A man. With a heart. With a conscience. With regrets and accomplishments. A man with a history.

But as he lay there, eyes half-glazed with weariness, Ryan had a hard time making that history black. Or white. There were definite dark smudges. And there were twenty years of service and goodness. Compassion and striving. Twenty years of near perfection.

More than he could say for himself.

At best, he'd give himself…

Zero.

He was a bigoted, unrelenting, judgmental ass.

So…there. He'd arrived. He knew who he was. And with the knowing came a measure of peace. Ryan's muscles settled, falling into the softness of his mattress, letting it cradle him. Hold him.

And…

The knocking started on his head. If he didn't get some sleep, the headache that had been plaguing him for days was going to drive him to the point of insanity. As it was, it knocked incessantly. Preventing sleep. Here he was, in a cloud of cotton, being tended to all around by little white beings, and still the knocking continued, like some black vapor, pounding at him, preventing nirvana.

It hurt.

And grew louder.

Swearing, sitting up, ready to take on the vapor, to show it he was still boss, Ryan woke up with a start.

And realized that his head didn't hurt at all. A quick glance at the clock told him he'd been out almost twenty-four hours.

And the knocking—it was at his front door. Pulling on a

pair of shorts as he hopped for the stairs, Ryan made himself decent and ran the rest of the way to the door.

Too disoriented to figure out who he was expecting, he had a quick apology on his tongue, a planned request for a shower, as he pulled open the door.

"Do you always sleep this late?"

He had an appointment with Amanda Lincoln? Didn't seem like that was something he'd forget.

"I work nights," he said.

"Thursday night was your last shift. This is Saturday."

Right. "I'm sorry." The woman seemed to ~~confused~~ the response. He was sorry. A sorry-assed fool.

"Well, you weren't expecting me so I can hardly expect a welcome. But I'd like a few minutes of your time, just the same."

"Of course." It didn't even occur to Ryan to argue. Or to wonder why, in light of the fact that he and Audrey were over, her mother would have any business with him. "Give me fifteen minutes to shower and—"

"I've been knocking for five." Amanda glanced at her watch. "I can give you a couple of minutes to put on some clothes. The shower isn't necessary. I'm not anyone you need to impress."

He'd been thinking of waking up, feeling human, but Ryan didn't see any good to come from pointing that out. He nodded, left the door open for her to make her own way in and took the stairs two at a time.

"HE HASN'T CALLED, Delilah girl. Guess you were an oversight, too. Another one he pretended to care about who he can cut off at the quick without a second glance. We're better off without him."

Delilah purred. Snuggled up to Audrey's chin and went back to sleep. They'd been that way most of the week. On the couch, with the television on, but muted, taking solace from each other.

She'd gone to work. And to lunch with her mother. And she'd come home to Delilah.

"You saved my life, you know," she said to the sleeping cat. "If you hadn't come walking out that first night and kissed me, I don't know what I'd have done."

Tears filled her eyes, as they'd been doing all week.

"How long does this grief process take?" she asked the all-knowing feline. And wished, for the hundredth time, Delilah could actually impart her wisdom. "We've got to get up. Get out. Get busy."

Doing what she didn't know. But doing something.

"It's Saturday morning. The sun is shining. What do you say we take a walk?"

Delilah didn't like walks. She didn't like to leave the house.

Which was fine with Audrey. She didn't feel like leaving, either.

"YOU DON'T MAKE bad coffee."

"Thank you."

"I didn't come to discuss your coffee. Or even to have any."

Dressed in a skirt and light, short-sleeved blazer, with tasteful gold jewelry and enough makeup to enhance her natural beauty, Amanda Lincoln looked ready for a designer showroom.

"Why are you here?" he asked, comfortable with her tactics. Up front and in your face. It was about all Ryan was capable of first thing in the morning. Without a shower.

Or any other time, these days.

"I have something to tell you. I've known there would be a day when I would have to tell my secret. I just didn't know when. After seeing my daughter yesterday for the lunch we were all three supposed to have together, I was impressed with the notion that the time had come. I gave it overnight and woke with the same conviction this morning."

She was talking conviction. A concept he could understand. With a sip of strong coffee, he motioned her to continue.

"Leonard Wilson is Audrey's father."

Ryan choked. Spilled hot coffee on his thigh. And more on the carpet when he jumped up. Dropping the cup in the kitchen sink with one hand, while turning on the cold water with the other, he accepted the towel being handed to him without question.

Third-degree burns were painful. And he was in enough pain.

SHE'D MADE IT to the shower. Had dried her hair. Sprayed it. Managed foundation. And it was only noon. At this rate, she'd have mascara on by five. Time enough to begin reversing the process in preparation for bed.

Audrey needed her rest. Tomorrow she was going to return Delilah to her owner. With a request that he sign over adoption papers.

In the process, she was going to give Ryan Mercedes a piece of her mind. Assuming she had any left. It was disappearing by the hour.

But at least she wasn't crying. She'd gone two hours with no moisture other than the shower. Decided improvement. Worth celebration. She'd skip lipstick as a reward.

Her cell phone rang and she glanced toward the bedroom, but didn't move.

And maybe ignore the phone, too.

It rang again.

Or maybe not. It could be one of her kids.

"Hello?" She was out of breath, hadn't had time to check caller ID on the screen before her voicemail was due to pick up.

"Hi."

It was him. She'd waited for days. Too many days. That made her mad.

"What do you want?"

"Just to let you know I'm in the kitchen. I put a pot of coffee on."

"What, why?"

"Because I haven't had any. I spilled mine all over myself, had to take a shower to clean it off and didn't want to wait to make another pot."

What on earth was he babbling about?

"Why are you in my kitchen?"

"I told you. I needed coffee."

Audrey exhaled, lifting her bangs off her forehead. Exasperating her at this point wasn't wise. She was apt to start bawling.

Stopping could take most of the afternoon.

"How'd you get in my house?"

"Your mother gave me her key."

Weird was getting surreal. "My mother."

"Yes."

"When did you see my mother?"

"This morning."

She tried the harder question again. "Why?"

"Because she came over. Woke me up, actually. I'd been out for almost twenty-four hours."

That pissed her off, too. Here she'd been, too broken up to sleep for more than an hour at a time, and then it had been sleep fraught with nightmares—and he'd been blissfully unconscious for a whole day.

Ready to give him a real piece of her mind, to send him to hell and take her life back, Audrey said, "I'm coming out."

"I was hoping you'd say that."

"Don't mess with me, Ryan. You aren't on my good side."

"Point taken. There's a cup of coffee waiting for you."

Hanging up, Audrey gave Delilah one last stroke. "I'm just going out there to secure your future," she whispered. "I'll be back before you know it and you'll never have to go back to that…that…"

Unable to come up with a word that properly described what she and Delilah thought of Ryan Mercedes, Audrey left it to the higher being of the two of them and walked slowly out to her kitchen.

SHE LOOKED exhausted. Dark shadows under her eyes, hair straight and hanging around her as if its weight was too heavy to bear. An old pair of shorts and a tank top. No shoes.

Ryan had to physically hold himself back from pulling her into his arms and keeping her there forever.

"I'm sorry," he said before she was even fully in her seat. He'd taken a seat on the side of the table. She'd chosen the end next to him. He wasn't sure what that meant. If anything. Just noticed, anyway.

"Apology accepted." She was sipping coffee as though

she hadn't a care in the world, and Ryan might have panicked if not for the fact that she was avoiding his gaze.

She wouldn't be doing that if he didn't still have some effect on her.

"I was wrong."

"Yes."

"I'd like your forgiveness." His honesty wasn't getting through to her. "Let me rephrase that. I need your forgiveness."

"You have it." Her glare pinned him. "Now is that all?"

"No, I—"

"If you think you're going to walk back in here, with or without my mother's support, you're dumber than I thought, Mercedes. You, with all your promises. Your avowals of unconditional love and talk about the bigger picture, about eternity and forever and a bond that surpasses this surface human life. You're full of shit. Now get out and leave me alone."

He deserved her anger. "I made the biggest mistake of all," he said aloud, thinking of Amanda. And Mark. Of Takeisha. Of Audrey. "I felt the love. I knew it was there. And I walked away from it."

The realization stunned him. Floored him. Staring at Audrey as the lifeline she was in that moment, his one attachment to reality, he felt the flood of shame, of regret. Of knowing he'd screwed up and there was absolutely nothing he could do to take back his actions.

"When my critical moment came, I chose to live by my head, not my heart."

She didn't relent. Didn't give him anything at all. And he didn't blame her.

"I can't believe it."

Standing, Ryan pushed in his chair with precise care. Grabbed his keys. Dropped hers on the table and walked to the door.

"Wait just a damned minute, buster."

He stopped as the venom hit him in the back of the head.

"If you think you're going to casually walk away from me a second time, you'd better reconsider. I'm not having it."

Turning, Ryan stared at the tornado coming at him. Her face was red. Her arms were flailing. Her fists clenched. He had only enough time to raise his arms to deflect her blows. They came at him one after another. Not hard blows. Not bruising or damaging blows.

Not even blows he couldn't prevent. He could have grabbed her wrists at any time. He didn't.

Those fists striking him were symbolic. He deserved this.

And if fate had kept a tally, they could be at this a long, long time.

HER ANGER had long since been depleted, and still Audrey pounded at Ryan's chest. How long was he going to stand there and take it? How long could she keep it up?

Where did they go from here?

Out of the corner of her eye she saw Delilah walk in. And suddenly the words came to her.

"Take me in your arms, idiot." Had she really said that?

Before she could follow the thought any further, Ryan's arms were around her and all thought fled. He clutched her so hard it hurt. His heart pounded against her until she couldn't tell what was his life beat and what was hers. And without warning, before she could even try to stop herself, she started to sob.

THEIR LOVEMAKING was hot. Desperate. Wet with tears. And completely silent. Ryan entered Audrey without gentleness, just as she rose to meet him with a force she'd never shown before. He kissed her, mating their tongues, their mouths, their breath. He touched her breasts. Her nipples. Touching her everywhere that was intimate. That was his.

Pumping in and out of her, he started to cry—something he couldn't remember ever doing before. Tears filled his eyes, dripped down his cheeks, and still he thrust forward, withdrew and thrust again.

She was his. He was hers. Period.

There was no other option.

"THANK YOU."

Not bothering to lift her head from his chest, Audrey asked, "For what?" It was early yet. Ryan had only been there half an hour or so, but a lifetime had passed.

A life of aloneness.

"For this."

This? As in sex? Lying naked on the living-room floor together? Or the deeper this? The one that rewrote her definitions of herself.

"It took you long enough."

"What does that mean?"

Maybe if she wasn't so tired this would be easier.

"To get back here."

Ryan's hand running lightly across her shoulder blade froze. "You knew I'd be back."

"In my rational moments. You left Delilah."

His hand started to move again. And Audrey knew she had to be completely honest.

"I know you, Ryan. One of the key characteristics that makes you you, that makes you so special to me, is that you *do* live by your heart. I didn't. At all. Until you, I let fear of repeated hurts, of not measuring up, control my life. I made all my decisions consciously, logically. I didn't trust my heart."

She was out of breath, her lungs squeezed with emotions set free from the unnatural chains that had bound them all these years. "You changed all of that," she told him. "You, my soul mate, recognized me on that deeper level you talk about. And I, in spite of myself, recognized you. The other day, you were me. Scared to death. Acting from your head as a means to try to prevent the emotions from overwhelming you. Trying to control what can't be controlled. And when I saw myself in you, when I saw how wrong you were, how much you were hurting yourself, I saw me. A lifetime of me. A me I don't want to be."

She waited. Expected some argument. She had it on the best authority—her own experience—this stuff was hard to take.

"You're right."

"That's it?"

"That's it. You are one hundred percent completely right and I feel like a first-class fool. I let you down. I let me down."

In spite of the seriousness of their conversation, Audrey couldn't help but smile. This was so Ryan.

"Welcome back, my friend," she said.

Shaking his head, Ryan lined her lips with his finger. "I am so sorry, Audrey. Here I thought I was all grown-up and a match for you or any man any age, and I was acting like a little kid."

"Hey, big boy." Lifting herself up on one elbow, she tweaked his chin. "Don't be so hard on yourself. You're human just like the rest of us. Welcome to the imperfect world of human existence."

RYAN COULDN'T GET enough of her. Of love. Of living. He made love to Audrey again because there was no other way to accept and communicate the depth of passion raging through him. Gently this time. In the bed. And in the shower, he washed her, every inch of her, discovering the eternal gift she was. Vowing to himself, to the gods, to whatever powers there were, that he was going to be faithful to the life he'd been given.

"We're still going to have tough issues to face," he said, watching as the water ran over her breasts. "You're thirteen years older than I am and people are bound to make remarks."

"I know."

"And you're going to have moments when you think that you aren't pretty enough for me anymore."

"I know."

She was too calm. Too accepting. Ryan watched her. "You're sure you're okay with that?"

He couldn't pretend anymore. Couldn't live with the fear of losing her.

"What I'm sure of is that no matter how hard it is living with you, it's harder living without you. I found that out firsthand."

Ryan hadn't thought she'd find words to reassure him; he'd expected it to take time, lots of it. And here he was, feeling the chains of fear break away, leaving him light and young and strong and ready.

"I'm going to make mistakes," he reminded her just to be sure, as he turned the hand sprayer toward her shoulders.

"Of course you are. I am, too. And you're going to have to deal with that."

"I'm going to be thankful for your mistakes for the rest of my life," he said, not sure he'd ever again be able to truly see anything Audrey did as wrong. She'd have a reason. And he'd love her enough to see it.

"Why is that?"

"Because they allow me mine."

Maybe it was a twisted way of thinking, but it worked for him. And apparently for her, too, judging by the way she was inching her mouth up toward his.

THEY WERE IN the kitchen, midafternoon, making peanut-butter-and-jelly sandwiches before Audrey remembered something.

"You came over here for a specific purpose this morning," she said, licking jelly off her knife. "With my mother's key," she added. "What was that about?"

Her heart stopped a moment, all joy on hold, as Ryan's hands stilled above the slice of bread.

"Let's sit down." Taking her hand, he left the half-made sandwiches on the counter and led her to the table.

"What?"

Was her mother dying? Had he come out of pity?

"Your mother came to tell me something that she should be telling you herself, but in her strange way, she's turning you over to me. Giving up her control, she says. She knew the time would come when she would have to let you go and that when that time came, there was something you had to know."

This sounded ominous. Audrey wasn't ready for anything else.

Ryan took her hand. She concentrated on the strength that existed from their togetherness.

"Sweetie, your mother has been lying to you, to everyone, for your entire life."

"How?"

"Leonard *is* your father."

Shocked, Audrey stared at him. Words of denial sprang to mind, but quickly faded. To be replaced by a sense of knowing that brought a peculiar calm to her heart.

She jumped up, knocking her chair over. "How could she do that? How could she keep him from me? Keep me from him? Why?"

"The answer's simple really." Ryan's voice brought sanity to an insane moment, reality into desperation. "She *was* in love with Jeff. She wanted to marry him. But they hadn't slept together. When your father started talking about those psychological examinations, she panicked. What if it was found out that she really was whacked?" Ryan grabbed Audrey's hand, pulled her down to his lap. "Her word, not mine," he said. "She got it into her head that they were going to lock her up, institutionalize her or put her on meds that would make her into a zombie. So she told your father about Jeff, taking away any right he had to look out for your best interests. And then Jeff died, and she saw the writing on the wall where your father and Becky were concerned, and somehow worked it out in her mind that it was all for the best. Your father and Becky could have their own family. And she'd have you."

"But what about *me?*" Embarrassed when she heard the

little-girl plea in her voice, Audrey continued, "I mean, what about my right to have a father?"

"Your mother's father was abusive, she says."

"That's right."

"She grew up without the love of a father and didn't think the loss of a father's love was as bad for you as being split between two families would have been."

"Do Leonard and Becky know this?"

"No, she said she'd wait to hear from you on how you want to handle telling him. She said to tell you she's willing to meet with them if you'd prefer it happen that way."

"I want to tell them, I think. But only if you'll be there."

"Of course I will be."

"He's my dad," she said, resting her head against Ryan's chest, a little girl and a grown woman both at once. The two of them coming together inside her, completing her. "I have a dad. And he's a good man. And he wants me."

"That's right, sweetie." Ryan's voice above her was soft and filled with compassion.

"We have to go there," she said. "But not yet. Not today."

She needed today—a day to be with the love of her life, to solidify all that they were to each other, to focus on Ryan and the woman she was, the life she had, before she went back to the beginning.

"You name the time," he said. "I just have one stipulation."

Pulling back, looking up at him, Audrey asked, "What?"

"We don't go anywhere to meet anyone until we get a diamond for that finger."

"Which finger?"

"The one that's going to wear my wedding ring just as soon as we can get a license."

"Oh, that finger." Laughter bubbled inside her. Mixed with the purest joy. And total exhaustion. "Is that a proposal, Mercedes?"

"Yes."

"You're going to have to work on that. An older man would have had more finesse. He'd have gotten down on his knees and—"

His lips cut off her words right when she was really getting going. And they kept her occupied for the next hour, in the next room on the couch she'd shared with Delilah all week, crying for Ryan.

And when they were spent, when they'd made love, spoken of love and promised a lifetime of love, she laid her head on Ryan's shoulder, took a deep breath, and finally, after a lifetime of fighting demons in the dark, fell peacefully to sleep.

* * * * *

*Ladies, start your engines with a sneak preview
of Harlequin's officially licensed
NASCAR® romance series.*

Life in a famous racing family comes at a price

All his life Larry Grosso has lived in the shadow of
his well-known racing family—but it's now time for
him to take what he wants. And on top of that list is
Crystal Hayes—breathtaking, sweet...and twenty-two
years younger. But their age difference is creating ani-
mosity within their families, and suddenly their
romance is the talk of the entire NASCAR circuit!

*Turn the page for a sneak preview of
OVERHEATED
by Barbara Dunlop
On sale July 29 wherever books are sold.*

Rufus, as Crystal Hayes had decided to call the black Lab, slept soundly on the soft seat even as she maneuvered the Softco truck in front of the Dean Grosso garage. Engines fired through the open bay doors, compressors clacked and impact tools whined as the teams tweaked their race cars in preparation for qualifying at the third race in Charlotte.

As always when she visited the garage area, Crystal experienced a vicarious thrill, watching the technicians' meticulous, last-minute preparations. As the daughter of a machinist, she understood the difference a fraction of a degree or a thousandth of an inch could make in the performance of a race car.

She muscled the driver's door shut behind her and waved hello to a couple of familiar crew members in their white-and-pale-blue jump suits. Then she rounded the back of the truck and rolled up the door. Inside, five boxes were marked Cargill Motors.

One of them was big and heavy, and it had slid forward a few feet, probably when she'd braked to make the narrow parking lot entrance. So she pushed up the sleeves of her canary-yellow T-shirt, then stretched forward to reach the box. A couple of catcalls came her way as her faded blue jeans tightened across her rear end. But she knew they were good-natured, and she simply ignored them.

She dragged the box toward her over the gritty metal floor.

"Let me give you a hand with that," a deep, melodious voice rumbled in her ear.

"I can manage," she responded crisply, not wanting to engage with any of the catcallers.

Here in the garage, the last thing she needed was one of the guys treating her as if she was something other than, well, one of the guys.

She'd learned long ago there was something about her that made men toss out pickup lines like parade candy. And she'd been around race crews long enough to know she needed to behave like a buddy, not a potential date.

She piled the smaller boxes on top of the large one.

"It looks heavy," said the voice.

"I'm tough," she assured him as she scooped the pile into her arms.

He didn't move away, so she turned her head to subject him to a *back off* stare. But she found herself staring into a compelling pair of green...no, brown...no, hazel eyes. She did a double take as they seemed to twinkle, multicolored, under the garage lights.

The man insistently held out his hands for the boxes. There was a dignity in his tone and little crinkles around his eyes that hinted at wisdom. There wasn't a single sign of flirtation in his expression, but Crystal was still cautious.

"You know I'm being paid to move this, right?" she asked him.

"That doesn't mean I can't be a gentleman."

Somebody whistled from a workbench. "Go, Professor Larry."

The man named Larry tossed a "Back off" over his shoulder. Then he turned to Crystal. "Sorry about that."

"Are you for real?" she asked, growing uncomfortable with the attention they were drawing. The last thing she needed was some latter-day Sir Galahad defending her honor at the track.

He quirked a dark eyebrow in a question.

"I mean," she elaborated, "you don't need to worry. I've been fending off the wolves since I was seventeen."

"Doesn't make it right," he countered, attempting to lift the boxes from her hands.

She jerked back. "You're not making it any easier."

He frowned.

"You carry this box, and they start thinking of me as a girl."

Professor Larry dipped his gaze to take in the curves of her figure. "Hate to tell you this," he said, a little twinkle coming into those multifaceted eyes.

Something about his look made her shiver inside. It was a ridiculous reaction. Guys had given her the once-over a million times. She'd learned long ago to ignore it.

"Odds are," Larry continued, a teasing drawl in his tone, "they already have."

She turned pointedly away, boxes in hand as she marched across the floor. She could feel him watching her from behind.

* * * * *

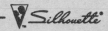

SPECIAL EDITION

A late-night walk on the beach resulted
in Trevor Marlowe's heroic rescue of a
drowning woman. He took the amnesia
victim in and dubbed her Venus, for the
goddess who'd emerged from the sea.
It looked as if she might be his goddess of
love, too…until her former fiancé showed
up on Trevor's doorstep.

Don't miss

THE BRIDE WITH NO NAME

by *USA TODAY* bestselling author
MARIE FERRARELLA

*Available August
wherever you buy books.*

REQUEST YOUR FREE BOOKS!
2 FREE NOVELS PLUS 2 FREE GIFTS!

HARLEQUIN®

Super Romance®

Exciting, emotional, unexpected!

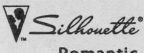

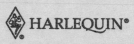

HARLEQUIN®

Cathy McDavid
Cowboy Dad
The State of Parenthood

Natalie Forrester's job at Bear Creek Ranch
is to make everyone welcome, which is an
easy task when it comes to Aaron Reyes—the
unwelcome cowboy and part-owner. His
tenderness toward Natalie's infant daughter
melts the single mother's heart. What's not
so easy to accept is that falling for him means
giving up her job, her family and the only
home she's ever known....

Available August
wherever books are sold.

LOVE, HOME & HAPPINESS

www.eHarlequin.com   HAR75225

Silhouette Desire

LAURA WRIGHT

FRONT PAGE ENGAGEMENT

Media mogul and playboy Trent Tanford is being blackmailed *and* he's involved in a scandal. Needing to shed his image, Trent marries his girl-next-door neighbor, Carrie Gray, with some major cash tossed her way. Carrie accepts for her own reasons, but falls in love with Trent and wonders if he could feel the same way about her— even though their mock marriage was, after all, just a business deal.

**Available August
wherever books are sold.**

Always Powerful, Passionate and Provocative.

HARLEQUIN Super Romance

COMING NEXT MONTH